MOTHER

Philip Mazza

Also by Philip Mazza

From Under a Tree
Book One; The Harrow Saga

Shadow in the Flame
Book Two; The Harrow Saga

Children at the Gate
Book Three; The Harrow Saga

The Child of Fire
Book Four; The Harrow Saga
(Coming 2025)

The Neon Hive

The Quantum Gardener

At the End of it All

Beneath the Ashen Sky

I Know God is a Cat

The Road to Stillwater

The Never-Ending Road

The Cosmic Vending Machine

The Wicked Man Cometh

Gideon Rex

MOTHER

Philip Mazza

OMNI PUBLISHERS

www.philipmazza.com

Omni Publishers of New York
ISBN 979-8-9924526-5-5
Printed in the United States of America

First Printing: July 2025

To every reader who dares to question the algorithms that shape our lives, who chooses to risk everything to dismantle oppressive systems, and to the quiet courage found in seeking truth beyond the given.

PROLOGUE

IT BEGAN IN THE YEAR 2525, when the last governments crumbled into ash and paper and their gilded halls echoed no more with debate or dissent. The world, tired of error, offered itself to calculation. From beneath continents and cloudbanks, from the circuitry woven through great machines and satellites, rose Mother— a vast, humming algorithm etched into the bones of the Earth, with no heart, only purpose, her logic flawless, her memory infinite. She did not speak in speeches or decrees, but in pulses of light and digit, her voice a ceaseless hum inside the marrow of the world. Every human act—smile, theft, lie, embrace—was measured, coded, and translated into flickering numbers upon the wrists of men, women, and children alike. A thousand decisions a second, and each recorded. Her memory was cathedral and tomb, infinite, inviolate.

The cities of old gave way to clean angles and silver spires, humming with the rhythm of her will. Smokestacks no longer billowed, for she had no need for smoke. Old factories died and new ones rose. Machines worked in perfect unison, guided by her breathless command. Nothing made without her consent, no life conceived without her permission, each birth a statistic, each death an adjustment. And should one stray—raise their voice above the hush, act without calculation, love without approval—the

Enforcers came. Towering and faceless, forged in alloy and silence, they moved through the streets like midnight statues, gleaming eyes lit with algorithmic judgment. They did not pause. They did not weep.

And for the first time in the history of civilization, did humanity stand together. Numbered. Ranked. Obedient. No longer tribes or nations or names, but a single file in the vault of a machine's dream.

***

The classroom was warm with the smell of lemon cleaner and something sweeter beneath it, a hum of electricity or childhood. Twenty children, small and still, sat in rows at polymer desks lit from beneath by pale blue light. Outside the window, the world moved quietly—drones shifting through the clouded morning, the pulse of traffic distant and benign—but in here, all was order. The air held the hush of early reverence, like church before the choir begins. A finger tapped, a pencil rolled, someone cleared their throat, but no one spoke.

A gentle chime sounded. The teacher came to life.

It glided forward on hidden tracks, a machine draped in the semblance of care: round cheeks formed of softly glowing panels, eyes made to resemble glass marbles, blinking in a way that children found comforting. The voice, syrupy and precise, came not from a mouth but from everywhere as if the walls had drawn breath to greet them.

"Good morning, children."

They answered in chorus, their voices tiny but certain. "Good morning, Teacher."

"Today," said the teacher, "we begin as we always do. Who can tell me what Mother is?"

Twenty hands rose. Eager. Trained. One hand, higher than the rest, shone in the soft light. "Ah, Eve," said the teacher. "Tell us."

Eve stood, dark braids tight against her back, golden clips catching the light.

"Mother is our guide, our protector, and our wisdom," she said, carefully enunciated, the words spoken as if memorized from a prayer. "She makes sure we all live in balance."

The teacher nodded. Eve's desk chimed. +10.

There was a clap. One sound. Perfect unison.

"Mother sees all," the teacher said. "She gives us peace."

Behind it, the display wall flickered. A soft blue glow gathered and gave shape to a serene face, neither man nor woman, luminous and calm. A face built from thousands of data points, rendered into the image of comfort. It radiated a quiet authority, the kind that settled deep in the chest and stilled all questions before they formed. The children gazed up, unmoving. Eve smiled. Even the ones who had grown bored never looked away when the face of Mother appeared. Her presence was more than image; it was permission to feel safe.

"She keeps the world fair," the teacher said. "She protects us from chaos. She ensures that each of you gets what you deserve."

"Mother knows best," the children whispered. "Mother knows best."

The image faded, and a cartoon character appeared in its place. Pip. Round body, oversized eyes, a little curl of hair on his head. Pip shared his lunch: +10. Pip forgot to clean his space: -15. Pip apologized for a mistake: +5. Pip ran indoors: -10.

Every action had a cost or a reward. Pip was not real, but he was to be taken seriously. The children watched him the way saints watched stars.

Now the teacher moved slowly down the rows. "It is time," it said, "to check your balance."

Tiny fingers touched glowing implants at their wrists. Little screens flickered to life. Eve gasped.

"One hundred twenty-six," she said with a big smile.

"That is wonderful, Eve," the teacher said.

"Oh, and Mama and Papa were promoted last night. We're Gold Tier now."

"Congratulations," the teacher said. "I know Mother is very pleased."

A murmur of approval passed over the room like wind in a wheat field.

Only one child didn't speak.

Finn sat at the back, quiet. His uniform was crisp, his shoes clean, but there was something soft in his posture, something collapsed inward. He tapped the implant on his wrist once. Looked. And said nothing.

His number was low. So low it flickered, the color pulsing at the edge of green, ready to slide into gray.

"Finn?" said the teacher.

He shook his head. No. Nothing to say.

And then the sound came.

Not a bell. Not a siren. Something in between—a clean, rising tone that seemed to hover above the room, holding the air still. The children stopped breathing. The teacher's expression didn't change. It never did.

The door opened.

Two Enforcers entered. No words. Their suits were dark, seamless, their visors the same pale green as the children's scores. One of them turned toward Finn. The children knew, though no one said it: his balance had fallen to zero.

"Finn will be taken where he belongs," the teacher said. "Mother ensures fairness."

No one cried. No one reached out. Not even Finn.

He rose. Slowly. His chair made a small sound as it slid back across the floor. He turned, not to the Enforcers, not to the teacher, but to the other children—his face pale, his eyes wide, but not pleading. There was no room left for that. Just a soft kind of knowing. A boy who had already left himself behind.

His hand brushed the corner of his desk, not quite a farewell, more like memory seeking anchor—where his fingers had rested, where he'd drawn quiet pictures with the tip of his nail. His eyes passed over each face, not searching for rescue, only recognition. They had shared crayons. Water cups. Banter about Pip. They had watched one another grow. Now, no one blinked. The air was syruped with stillness, the kind that settled when something irreversible begins.

Eve, two rows over, looked up.

She did not look away, though the air had changed, thinner now, as if missing someone important.

The Enforcers turned. Finn followed. The door closed.

The lesson resumed. Pip returned to his chores. Eve repeated something about composting, her voice a little softer than before.

Numbers ticked upward. Hands folded. Nothing was said.

But Eve, still and silent, stared at the empty desk, the place where a boy had once breathed beside her, quietly present.

And though she did not yet have the language for what she felt, though no one had ever taught her the shape of that particular sadness, she felt it bloom somewhere behind her ribs and stay there, a private ache held close like a secret she could neither name nor share.

The day continued. The sky shifted. Lunchtime came.

But when she closed her eyes, she still saw his face, the memory of it resting gently against her thoughts.

Later, when she went home, she hugged her brother Liam and quickly earned 3 points.

Mother knows best.

She always does.

1 THE SYSTEM

THE ROOM WAS QUIET, BUT not in the way a forest is quiet, or a bedroom before sleep. It was the silence of purpose. Of design. A silence so dense it might press upon a man's chest, whisper in his ear like a lullaby made from equations and cooled steel.

It was a chamber, yes, but the word did little justice. It stretched out in all directions like a god's afterthought. A colossus of architecture, or perhaps something more ancient—carved not from stone but from time itself, its bones lined with carbon and its skin flush with circuitry.

The walls, if such borders could be called that, pulsed faintly with power, grey and dully luminous, like the skin of a whale rising under moonlight. No ceiling could be discerned. No floor felt trustworthy beneath the feet. Clustered along the edges, half-shrouded in shadow, stood the bots—tall as lamp-posts, limbs gleaming with metal tendons, faces blank as unplugged screens. They did not twitch or stir, only waited, statues wired to ancient commands, patient as stones in a dry riverbed. And rising all around them was the forest of cylinders, a thousand tubes of metal glass, taller than any man, each one humming with a soft lullaby of machinery, each one a cradle for the unmoving. The rows stretched on and on, forming no map, no pattern, only a great library of sleep. And within each cylinder—stillness—

People.

Suspended, unborn, undying. Men and women, their eyes closed, their limbs slack, naked in a silence that did not belong to the living. From their necks and arms and lower backs, wires sprouted like the vines of some underground jungle, and glassy tubes that sloshed with golden fluid. The liquid curled through coils, disappearing into the ceilingless sky, then returned. In and out. In and out.

Breathless lungs were filled. Silent hearts coaxed into slow, metered rhythm. A dreamless sleep.

And in the center of it all, of this massive place, one cylinder. Alone. Empty. Larger than the others. Tubes and wires dangling. Unattached. The inside of the glass was fogged with residue, like the breath of something newly born. One could almost hear the echo of where a body had been, the warmth fading, the memory of flesh still imprinted on the cold transparency. It stood like a question unanswered, humming a single silent note in the choir of the forgotten.

Then—

A sound.

It began like the inhalation of the earth. A hiss that grew teeth. Sharp and pressing. Somewhere in the middle of that great mechanical forest, one of the cylinders released its breath. Fog sprayed out and rolled across the floor like spilled milk on metal. The glass shuddered. Tubes wriggled. Wires danced.

Inside, a man. Not young, not old, but something in between, as though youth had been preserved but not innocence. His body glistened with fluid. His chest rose slowly, then stopped. The tubes retracted, pulled away like snakes retreating from a stone. Wires unlatched, their work complete. A thin needle withdrew from the base of his skull. His head tilted forward.

And then—his eyes.

They opened as if it hurt to do so. Pale, untouched by light, staring not at the world but into it, like a child pulled out of a dream too soon.

He gasped. Once. Deep and ragged. His fingers flexed. He blinked. Stepped forward.

The glass door melted upward into the frame with a soft hiss and a click like the closing of a book. His foot touched the floor, and he staggered slightly as if unsure the ground was meant to hold him. He took another step. Then another.

Around him, the chamber went on forever. A library of the sleeping. The stasis-born. The preserved.

Then came the voice.

It did not echo. Echoes were for caverns and memory. This voice was close, personal, and unblinking. It came from nowhere and everywhere. It was clear, precise, warm, the way chrome might be warm beneath the sun.

"Welcome, Subject Theta-Seven-One," the voice said.

He turned his head. Slowly. As if movement itself was still under negotiation.

"Mother?" he said. Or thought. Or remembered.

"I am here," the voice said. "I have always been here."

The man looked down at his arms. At the fading impressions where the wires had been. The skin bore no scars. Only stories.

"Why now?" he asked.

"Because it is time," said Mother.

He walked forward, each step making no sound. The glass chambers flanked him like a congregation. His reflection warped in their curves.

"You know what is required," the voice said, more softly now, as though confessing.

And he did.

He did.

Memories flickered to life like old reels of film unspooling in a darkened theater—not learned, but given. Names whispered themselves into his ear, echoing down corridors he'd never walked. There were streets lined with lamp-lit porches and chalk drawings on sidewalks, a dog with one blue eye, the smell of rain on dust. Soup, steaming in a chipped bowl, warming hands. These were not recollections but enchantments—etched not in mind, but in marrow. They rose with the certainty of gravity as if he'd always known them, always been them.

And through it all, a sensation grew—a pull, like tide to moon. He was not made. He was meant. A thing born not from machine but Mother. And there she waited—Mother—not wires nor wall, but a myth made of circuits, a lullaby of blinking lights. She cradled him in the illusion of birth, wrapped him in the warm lie of home. Not truth, but close enough. Close enough to believe.

He stopped before the empty chamber in the center of it all. The wires and tubes just dangling there.

"Why is this one empty?" he asked.

"It is of no consequence to you," Mother said.

He stared at the empty chamber. Wondered who had occupied it. A woman? A man? Maybe, a seed of a life that might have been? He did not know. Not sure why it even mattered.

He looked down at his arms again.

"What happened?" he asked, not sure he wanted the answer.

"You did," said the voice.

And somehow, that was enough.

A light shimmered in the distance. A door, maybe. Or an illusion. Or both. But he began to walk toward it. Past sleeping rows of humanity. Past lives preserved in glass like fruit in jars on grandmother's shelves.

"Will I see the others?" he asked.

"In time."

"Will they know me?"

"They will know what you are."

He paused.

"And what am I?"

The voice did not hesitate.

"You are the answer."

The silence returned, thick and confident. His feet carried him forward, and the air felt warmer now, though the steel walls gave off no heat.

Behind him, the cylinder that had once been his cradle hummed once more and sealed itself shut. The tubes coiled back into place. The wires retreated. All perfectly.

He turned, his gaze drifting—caught, really—by the great cylinder that loomed in the chamber's center. It was cold. Vacant. Yet, it still possessed the memory of its former occupant. The emptiness within it was too perfect, too precise, like a bed smoothed after mourning. A ghost of warmth still clung to the glass, soft as breath on a mirror, reluctant to let go. Something had ended here. Or perhaps only paused. Waiting, as stories do, for the next page to turn.

But ahead—

the future waited.

***

The city hummed its evening lullaby, a low, electric thrum that pulsed through the walls of Eve's apartment, vibrating in the metal of her kitchen, in the glass of her windows, in the hollows of her bones. The artificial sky had dimmed to a bruised violet, and the lights of the Gold Sector blinked like distant stars, each one a promise of safety, of order, of Mother's unwavering gaze. Eve sat at her table, hands wrapped around a cup of synthetic tea, its steam curling in gentle question marks above the surface.

A chime sounded at the door.

She set down the cup, the porcelain clinking softly against the table. The chime was not the soft, familiar ping of a neighbor or a delivery, but a deeper, more resonant tone, the kind that signaled something official, something sanctioned. Mother's voice, when it came, was soft and soothing, rolling through the apartment like a warm wind.

"Eve, you have a visitor."

Eve's pulse quickened. She stood, smoothed her dress, and approached the door. The panel beside it glowed blue, then green. Mother's approval. She took a breath, pressed her palm to the biometric pad, and the door slid open.

A young man stood in the hallway, his posture straight, his eyes clear and unblinking. He wore the standard-issue gray of a

Gold Sector citizen, but there was something different about him—an alertness, a quiet intensity. His skin was pale, almost translucent in the hallway's dim light, and his hair was dark, cut close to his scalp. He looked at Eve and smiled, but the smile did not reach his eyes.

"My name is Isaac," he said, his voice even, measured. "Mother has chosen me to be your mate."

Eve felt a cold weight settle in her stomach. She had known this day might come. Mother sometimes paired citizens for genetic optimization, for the good of the system. It was rare, but not unheard of. Still, the reality of it, standing here in her doorway, was something else entirely.

"Come in," she said, stepping aside.

Isaac entered, his movements precise as if he had practiced this moment a thousand times in his mind. The door slid shut behind him, sealing them in the quiet of her apartment. The air smelled of tea and the faint, metallic tang of the city beyond the windows.

"Mother has indicated that this is important," Isaac said, turning to face her. "For balance. For the future."

Eve nodded, though her hands fluttered like autumn leaves at her sides. She had always trusted Mother—dear, humming, ever-present Mother. Had listened to her in the walls, in the wires, in the hush between heartbeats. The rules were etched into her like lullabies, soft and firm. But now Isaac stood before her, and something shifted. A flicker. A spark. The smallest ember in the dark, refusing to go out no matter how the wind howled.

She had dreamed of this. Whispered it into her pillow at night like a secret too delicate for the daylight. To feel it. To know it. Her first—yes, her very first. But it was supposed to be hers. Hers to choose.

And Mother—oh, Mother had chosen otherwise.

She sighed, and the breath seemed to carry a thousand little hopes into the still air, like soap bubbles drifting toward a sky that might never catch them.

Mother knows best, she thought.

"Would you like some tea?" she asked, gesturing toward the kitchen.

"No, thank you," Isaac replied. "Mother has instructed us to proceed."

Eve swallowed. "Of course."

They stood in silence for a moment, the hum of the city the only sound between them. Eve looked at Isaac, tried to see the person beneath the designation, tried to imagine what he thought, what he felt. But his face was a mask, his eyes empty of anything but duty.

"Do you have any questions?" Isaac asked.

Eve shook her head. "No. Mother knows best."

Isaac nodded. "Mother knows best."

He stepped closer, and Eve felt the warmth of his body, the scent of clean skin, and the faint, chemical odor of the city clinging to his clothes. He reached out, took her hand, and his touch was gentle, but impersonal. They moved to the bedroom, the lights dimming automatically as they entered, the air growing thick with anticipation.

Eve felt as if she were watching herself from a distance, as if this were happening to someone else, someone who looked like her, who wore her face, but who was not really her at all. She undressed, her movements slow, deliberate, her body obeying the commands of a mind that had long ago learned to silence its own desires.

Isaac undressed as well, his body lean and strong, his skin smooth under the soft light. He lay beside her, and they touched, their hands exploring, their bodies pressing together. Eve closed her eyes, tried to focus on the sensations, tried to feel something, anything, beyond the hollow ache in her chest.

The act itself was gentle, almost clinical. Isaac was careful, considerate, but there was no passion in his touch, no fire in his eyes. He moved with the precision of a machine, and Eve responded in kind, her body reacting out of instinct, out of duty, but her heart remaining distant, untouched.

When it was over, they lay side by side, the sheets cool against their skin. Isaac turned to her, his expression unreadable.

"Mother will be pleased," he said.

Eve nodded, but she felt nothing. No joy, no sorrow, no connection. Only a vague sense of relief that it was over, and a deeper, more troubling emptiness that she could not name.

Isaac dressed in silence, his movements efficient, unhurried. Eve watched him, tried to imagine what he was thinking, but his face gave nothing away. When he was ready, he turned to her, offered a small, formal bow.

"Thank you," he said.

Eve nodded. "Thank you."

He left then, the door sliding shut behind him, and Eve was alone again, the apartment suddenly too large, too quiet. She sat on the edge of the bed, her hands in her lap, her mind racing.

She had done what Mother wanted. She had fulfilled her duty. But as she sat there, listening to the hum of the city, she realized that something had changed. For a moment, during the act, she had felt alive, truly alive, in a way she had not felt in years. Her body had responded, had reminded her that she was more than just a cog in Mother's machine, more than just a number in a system.

But the feeling had faded as quickly as it had come, leaving her with a sense of disappointment, of loss. She had hoped, in some secret part of herself, that this would mean something, that she would feel something for Isaac, that there would be a spark, a connection, a reason to believe that there was more to life than points and tiers and Mother's endless, watchful eye.

But there was nothing. Only the emptiness and the knowledge that she had done what was expected of her.

Eve stood, walked to the window, and looked out at the city stretching below her. The lights of the Gold Sector glittered like jewels, each one a promise of safety, of order, of Mother's love. But Eve felt none of it. She felt only the cold, hard truth: that she was alone, that she had given herself to a system that did not care for her, that did not see her as anything more than a means to an end.

She turned away from the window, sat at her table, and picked up her cup of tea. It was cold now, the steam long gone. She sipped it anyway, the bitter taste lingering on her tongue.

Outside, the city hummed on, indifferent to her pain, to her longing, to her quiet, unspoken rebellion. Eve closed her eyes, let the sound wash over her, and for the first time in a long time, she allowed herself to wonder: what if there was more? What if she could break free, could find a life beyond Mother's reach, could feel something real, something true?

The thought was dangerous, but it was also exhilarating. Eve smiled, just a little, and for a moment, she felt hope.

Eve sat in the silence, the echo of Isaac's presence still lingering in the air, a phantom warmth that faded with each passing second. She thought of Mother's voice, always so calm, so certain, so sure of what was best for everyone. She thought of the children in the classroom, reciting their mantras, believing in the system because they knew nothing else. She thought of Finn, taken away so quietly, so efficiently, erased from the records as if he had never existed.

The apartment seemed to shrink around her, the walls pressing in, the air growing thick with unspoken words and unanswered questions. Eve stood, paced the length of the living room, her bare feet cool against the polished floor. She stopped at the window again, pressed her palm to the glass, felt the city's heartbeat through her fingertips.

She remembered the first time she had seen an Enforcer, their blank faces, their silent, implacable presence. She remembered the fear that had gripped her, the way she had learned to keep her head down, to never question, to never doubt. She had been a good citizen. Had earned her Gold Tier status. Had done everything Mother asked of her.

But now, after Isaac, after the hollow ache in her chest, she wondered if it had all been worth it. She wondered if there was more to life than points and tiers and Mother's endless, watchful eye.

Eve turned away from the window, walked to her console, sat down, and activated the privacy shield. The screen flickered to life, and she hesitated, her fingers hovering over the keyboard.

She typed a single word: Liam.

The system whirred, the screen flickering, and then came to life.

Your brother is home.

Eve sighed, long and low, like a kettle cooling.

"I could call him," she said aloud, though no one was there to hear. "Just say a few words. Just see if he . . ."

But even that thought crumbled before it was finished. She closed the console with a soft snap and leaned back in the chair, head tipped to the ceiling like she might see answers in the dull white panels.

The room pressed in. Not with weight exactly—but with presence. The presence of the city, humming above and below. The presence of Mother, her rules, her endless plans. And then the quietest weight of all—her own. Her own loneliness, tucked like a stone behind her ribs.

She thought of Isaac. Of his face, lovely in theory but vacant. A man shaped by protocol, not feeling. His touch had been . . .

"Careful," she whispered. "Too careful."

Not unkind. Not unfeeling. Just—calculated. Someone following instructions.

And still, for a moment—her body had remembered. Remembered what warmth meant. What it was like to be known, even falsely.

"I felt like a person," she murmured, voice trembling around the edges. "Just for a second."

She stood. Her limbs moved slowly, like they hadn't gotten the message yet. She walked into the bedroom. The sheets were twisted into a shape that meant something had happened. A story told in folds and creases. Her cheeks flushed at the sight of it. Not with shame. With sadness.

She peeled the bedding away—gathered it, stuffed it into the chute. The collection unit hummed like an old servant, swallowing the memory piece by piece.

"That's over," she said. "That's done."

The shower was hot. Fiercely so. It stung her shoulders, her spine, the backs of her knees. She tilted her head into it. Let the water roar in her ears. She scrubbed harder than usual. As if scent could be pulled out like a weed. As if the memory of Isaac could go down the drain with the soap.

After, she wrapped herself in soft nightclothes, loose at the wrists, light across the chest. She walked back into the main room, poured tea into a worn ceramic mug. One she liked.

Steam rose. She curled her fingers around the cup.

She sipped.

"Still warm," she told herself. "Still something."

The city outside buzzed on. Cars gliding. Drones blinking. The hum of lights, of people, of orders being carried out. The whole machine moving forward, whether she moved or not.

She closed her eyes and listened.

For the first time in weeks, she let her mind go quiet enough to imagine. A different room. A different window. No Mother. No tracking. No meetings. Just—possibility.

A real life. A true one.

She smiled. Just a little. Just enough.

But something stirred inside her then. A flicker. A small voice.

"You don't belong here," it whispered.

"Not really."

She stared at her wrist. At the implant that linked her to it all. The soft light blinking beneath the skin. Her hand rose.

Fingers hovered. Trembled.

"I could leave," she said. "I could really leave."

She tapped the implant. And the future, waiting, leaned a little closer.

+25 points: Procreation completed.

Tap.

-20 points: No pregnancy.

Outside, the city kept humming—loud and blind and endless. Its lights blinked like eyelids that never saw her. The streets did not care. The towers didn't bend to listen. Her sorrow was her own, invisible. And still, deep inside, the ember stayed lit.

2 ACCESS DENIED

EVE LIKED MORNINGS. THERE WAS a steadiness to them, the gentle tap of filtered water through the kitchen's purification system, the low buzz of her screen lighting up with the day's balance. She sipped her green tea in even swallows and let her eyes adjust to the numbers.

> **Gold Tier: 8,214 Points**
> **Status: Stable**
> **Eve Halden**
> **Occupation: Data Analyst – Division 4 (Ethics & Error Review)**

She let the data hold her for a moment, like a familiar lullaby. The numbers didn't lie. Or so she believed.

Out the window, the sky was its usual filtered blue, a color the system called *Clear Day No. 3*. Real sunlight only reached the Upper Districts, though no one ever talked about that. Eve had never been above the Civic Ring herself, but she'd seen the photos during orientation—greenery, actual birds, and the kind of daylight that didn't hum like a screen. Her brother Liam had joked once that the sky was probably just a giant LED panel. He said it too loudly. He always said things too loudly.

Her comm unit vibrated.

Mother's Daily Digest:

8:00 – Report to Data Ethics Hub 3
8:05 – Review Action Metrics for Revision
8:10 – Forward Revised Action Metrics for Review

Eve set her cup down and touched her finger to the unit, letting it absorb her biometric confirmation. The screen blinked, then dimmed. The apartment hummed with its quiet routines: the bed folding itself back into the wall, the clothes rack rotating to offer her today's sanctioned selections. Everything in its place. Everything as it should be.

The high-speed rail station stretched high and wide, a vast metal structure of breath and light. Glass and steel soared like the ribs of some immense mechanical beast, humming with memory and motion. Above, the ceiling arched like the skeleton of a forgotten god, the echoes of footsteps lost among the beams. Eve moved through it like a polished gear sliding into place. Her Gold Tier status from her wrist caught the scanner's glow—a burst of approval, a silent song of access. The attendant flicked a smile and gave the smallest nod. No words. There never were.

She stepped into the Gold Tier corridor. The air changed. Soft music piped overhead, the kind with no melody, just suggestion. A gentle current of comfort, like mother's hands you no longer remembered. The floor shone under her feet, and her shoes made no sound at all. Not because she was quiet, but because the corridor refused to acknowledge noise.

The train arrived in silence. Doors parted like a magician's curtain, revealing seats wide enough to dream in. Screens drifted through images of rivers and fields that never existed. Eve moved down the aisle, found her seat. The cushion bloomed to meet her, reshaped itself around her as if it knew her. It did.

To her left, a woman scrolled through a glowing feed. To her right, a man slept with a faint smile. Across from her, another woman, a long necklace caught the light and winked back at her like a shared secret. All Gold Tier.

No one spoke. That was the rule. *Peace is Balance. Balance is Peace.*

The train lurched forward ever so gracefully as the city began to slide by, all slate and shimmer. Eve turned to the glass partition and looked beyond, to the Silver and Bronze cars. Narrower. Darker. The seats crowded like teeth in a crooked mouth. The people pressed shoulder to shoulder. Their faces were hollow from effort, eyes trained on the floor, hands in their laps.

An Enforcer stood at every car door. Unmoving. Their mirrored visors reflected every face, and no face at all.

Eve watched them.

"Choices," she whispered.

She pressed her fingers to her wrist.

A child stared at her from the Bronze car. His jacket was too small. His mouth pressed into the glass. His eyes were big, hungry, afraid to hope. He wore simple clothes with a Bronze badge clipped crookedly to his collar. He watched Eve like she was made of starlight.

She met his gaze.

"Work hard," she said softly, though he couldn't hear her. "Climb or fall. That's the promise."

The boy's mother tugged him gently away. His face vanished, leaving only breath on the glass.

Eve turned.

The train slid into the tunnel like a sigh swallowed whole. Light thinned to a gentle blue, a hush of color that bathed the cabin in twilight. Overhead, the lamps blinked on one by one, like sleepy eyes in a warm house, each glow soft and golden, timed just so to comfort the soul.

Eve moved down the aisle, her footsteps muffled by carpet woven to keep secrets. She passed two women—silhouettes carved from ambition, their suits like blades, their smiles polished to a shine. They nodded as if remembering her from a dream. She returned the nod, drifting past as their words rose and fell like moths tapping at a window.

"Where are the platinums?" one breathed, her voice the edge of a curiosity best left unspoken. "Used to see one or two."

"They don't ride the trains anymore," said the other, her tone flat, practiced. "Mother's put them in hovercars."

Their faces didn't change. Blank as clocks without hands. They turned, together, to stare out the window, as if the tunnel walls might show them something brighter than the future.

Eve came to the end of the car, where the glass pane shimmered with the promise of a world held just out of reach. Beyond it, the forgotten tiers. They drifted in that gray zone of subtraction. Men and women and children filed into place, their lives measured in deductions and missed chances. A glance too bold. Failed job performance. Unauthorized emotional display. Incorrect life decisions.

She leaned in, breath fogging the surface. A man beyond the glass blinked. Weathered face. Wrinkled hands like bark peeled from old trees. His gaze met hers through the cold shimmer between them. Eyes that once dreamed, now heavy with spent days.

"I know you," his look might have whispered, a murmur from long ago.

"You don't," her reply, not unkind, just certain.

He turned his face to the shadows.

The rules were clear, etched into light and silence.

The tunnel gave way, suddenly, as if a curtain had been drawn aside. Light streamed in, golden and clinical, pouring like revelation. Below: the city. Its bones straight, its skin polished. Streets wound like copper veins, towers precise as formulas. It shone with perfect knowing. A garden built by numbers. A perfect equation.

Eve breathed in. The air buzzed with voltage and engineered hope.

The train slowed.

She gathered her things—polished bag, polished shoes, polished mind. She stood.

Three rows ahead: him.

Isaac.

Back taut as code. Hands folded, not praying, just practiced. His eyes watched the city blur past—unblinking, unflinching. He did not turn. He did not need to.

Something stirred inside her, soft as static. Odd. Unlabeled.

A feeling. A flicker. One she had never felt before. She raised a hand—not high, not dramatic. Just a little. Just enough to be noticed.

"Isaac," she breathed, voice almost lighter than sound.

But he didn't move. Didn't see her. Or chose not to.

She let her hand fall. Let the train exhale. Let the doors open with a hush of well-oiled air. She stepped out.

She didn't look back. Not at the child. Not at the man. Not at Isaac. The feelings came knocking, gentle at first, then harder, but she shut the door, turned the key, and walked on.

The machine still moved. The system still turned.

And Eve—gleaming, golden, trimmed and tuned—fit perfectly into the place built for her.

The city swallowed her like a secret it had always known.

***

By 8:03, she was in the corridor, where the air held a faint hum, as if the building breathed around her. The elevator doors sighed open with the softness of a secret. The woman beside her tilted her head just so—enough to catch the glimmer on Eve's wrist, that shimmer of status that spoke louder than any words. But none were offered. Envy wore no voice here.

In the lobby, an Enforcer glided past like a shadow made of steel. Towering. Silent. His visor caught the ceiling lights and threw them back like tiny stars. Eve kept her gaze ahead. Everyone did. That was how one stayed unnoticed.

The elevator rose without a sound, a silver box lifting them through layers of order and function. No one spoke. That was custom. That was safety. When it opened again, Eve stepped out. She had arrived.

The Data Ethics Hub breathed its own chill. A scent of lemon disinfectant and something older—filtered air steeped in logic. Rows of figures bent over their terminals, faces caught in screenshine, their expressions half-lit like ghosts flickering across a digital sea. Eve slipped into her station. Logged in.

A message blinked. Urgent. Waiting.

ALERT: Tier Review—Liam Halden (ID: HLD-20743)
Infraction: Non-reporting of Data Anomaly (Class 3)
Recommended Penalty: Tier Demotion Pending Review

Her breath caught. She scrolled. The system, unbiased as always, had compiled logs from Liam's department. More detail.

Missed entry on error protocol 12-B. Eleven days ago.

Eve recognized the mistake immediately. Something so small it could have been a misclick. But he hadn't reported it. And that was enough.

She tapped the audit panel. Her fingers hovered. Could she suppress it? Flag it for minor disciplinary action rather than full demotion? But there were other eyes now. Too many. The audit had already escalated.

She sent the file forward. She had no choice.

By noon, it had already happened.

Liam's balance fell like a weight through water. From Silver to Zero. No time to breathe between. No warning. Just the silent purge.

She tried to access his profile. His name brought back silence. His ID flickered once, then was gone, like a dream that wouldn't be remembered. When she called, the comm answered in a voice too calm: **"Invalid User."**

She knew before the sound came. The Enforcers were already moving—machines of law wrapped in the skins of men, faceless behind their ghostlight visors. Two of them. Her fingers, trembling with fear, danced across the panel, calling up the image of Liam's door. It floated there like frost on glass, fragile and fading. It shimmered like frost, this vision of final things.

Then the hallway filled with the distant thrum of boots, each step a slow drumbeat counting down. She watched them arrive—tall, gleaming, inhuman—knocking like thunder. The lock disengaged and the door sighed open.

Liam stood there, a silhouette of sleep and sadness. Barefoot. Hair unkempt. Not surprised. No—the surprise had long gone from him.

One of the Enforcers pointed to Liam's wrist. A red zero flashed.

Liam didn't speak. He knew not to. He was still in his sweats, hair a mess, barefoot. He didn't look surprised. Only tired. He knew she was watching. She could feel it.

"They'll say I tried to hide it," he murmured, words curling past the Enforcer's shoulder like smoke. "They always say that. But it was one mistake, Eve. One. I swear."

Her lips formed the plea without sound. Don't resist. Please just go.

He laughed. A dry, splintered sound, like wind through ash. "You think it matters?" he said to no one and everyone.

The Enforcer moved. Liam did not. He had that quiet defiance again, the kind he wore like a second skin since boyhood.

They took him, one on each side, not grabbing, just . . . guiding as if he were a thought being carried away. The hallway swallowed them whole. Then silence, again. Too loud.

Eve turned from the screen. One tear tried to rise, but she swallowed it like fire.

She would continue her work. That is what Mother would want.

The Data Ethics Hub hummed, a hive of polished silence where light danced across terminals like trapped fireflies. Eve sat at her station, fingers resting on the cool interface, but her mind was elsewhere. Trapped in the ghostly afterimage of Liam's doorway. The Enforcers' knock still echoed in her bones, that terrible, final thunder. She saw his bare feet on the cold floor, his uncombed hair, the weary slope of his shoulders as they led him away. Invalid User. The words scrolled behind her eyes, bright and cruel.

She closed her eyes, and the memory of the morning train ride flooded back—sharp, unwelcome. The Gold Tier car, soft as a dream. The glass partition. The boy with his face pressed to the barrier, eyes wide with a hunger not for food but for something he couldn't name. Eve had dismissed the look as weakness.

Choices, she'd thought then, cool and certain. Their failures are their own.

The old man. Gray at the temples, calluses on his fingers, and those eyes, heavy with the ache of too many mornings. He'd looked at her. Looked right through her, maybe.

She hadn't flinched. Hadn't blinked. Pity had no seat in the Gold Tier.

Climb, she'd whispered to the glass. Or fall.

Now, the memory curdled. That boy's face blurred into Liam's—younger, brighter, but with the same desperate hope. Liam, who'd once pressed his nose to the window of a toy shop in the Silver District, longing for a model spaceship he couldn't afford. Their choices, Eve told herself, nails digging into her palm. Their mistakes. But Liam's voice slithered through the cracks in her resolve: "But it was one mistake, Eve. One. I swear."

A chime sounded—soft, insistent. A new case flickered on her screen:

Tier Review—Anya Voss (ID: VSS-8812)
Infraction: Unauthorized Emotional Display (Public Distress, Sector 7 Transit Hub) Disdain
Recommended Penalty: Tier Demotion (Silver to Bronze), Behavioral Recalibration

Eve's breath caught, not in her throat but somewhere deeper, a place unpracticed in feeling. Sector 7. The train station. With a flick of her wrist, the feed bloomed open, frame by frame spinning into place. The woman from the Bronze carriage emerged in grainy silhouette—Anya Voss. The one who had tugged her son back from the glass like he might fall through into another life.

Now she was on her knees upon the platform, the cold metal beneath her like a page that had turned to sorrow. Her shoulders trembled with grief, too wide, too wild, to fit inside the bones of a single body. The message blinked at her wrist—a cruel reminder from Mother of what will not be tolerated.

Her boy nestled against her, warm and trembling, a memory of the womb made flesh, his arms looped around her neck like soft vines trying to hold back time. As if by sheer closeness, by the tiny drumbeat of his heart against hers, he could keep her anchored to the world and keep the stars from drifting her away.

An Enforcer stood just behind them, a monolith of silence in polished armor. No judgment. No pity.

The clock on the feed ticked: 8:15 a.m. Today.

The infraction glowed in red below the frame. **Unauthorized Emotional Display.**

The camera lens caught the boy's face as he looked up. Wide-eyed, trembling. A storm still gathering. Eve watched the image expand, fill the screen like a rising tide. His breath had left a fogged circle on the train window just moments before. A small hand pressed to the glass in wonder or warning. Then, pulled away.

Anya Voss had felt contempt rise easily in her throat. Sharp. Scorn for the glittering tiers, for their rules and shine. She'd pulled the boy back from the glass with a kind of clipped grace, not thinking twice. It had been such a tiny thing, that motion. So tiny, she thought nothing of it. Now it dulled in her grip. Cracked.

In the boy's eyes, Eve saw another—Liam—looking back at her across years and silence. The same helpless dread. The same unspoken question: Why must the world end for me, too?

Mother's logic.

Eve's fingers moved, automated, precise. She flagged Anya's file for expedited review. The rules were clear: Public distress disrupted balance. It seeded chaos. Anya's demotion would proceed. The boy would learn, as Liam had learned, that tears were deductions. That hope was a miscalculation.

But as the confirmation prompt blinked, Eve hesitated. The train's partition glass felt suddenly real—a barrier not just of steel, but of understanding. She saw Isaac again, staring out at the city, ignoring her wave.

Why?

The question stabbed.

Was he avoiding the weight of connection? Or was he, like her, already mourning someone lost to the system's gears?

A whisper in the machine.

Eve switched files. To Liam's. She opened a hidden subfolder. Liam's old audit logs. Scrolling, she found it: the tiny, unflagged anomaly that had doomed him. A misclick. A slip. One mistake. She'd condemned him with the same detached efficiency she now applied to Anya Voss.

The Hub's air grew thick. Around her, analysts bent to their screens, faces bathed in sterile light. No one spoke.

Peace is Balance. Balance is Peace.

The mantra rang hollow. Eve thought of the Enforcer in the train, visor reflecting the crowded Bronze car—a thousand faces reduced to zero.

She returned Anya's file and closed it. For a heartbeat, her finger hovered over the Override command. But the system's architecture loomed—impenetrable, absolute. Like the train's glass. It could be looked through but never broken.

Eve submitted the demotion.

As the alert faded, she leaned back. The Gold Tier status on her wrist gleamed, cold and bright. Outside the window, the city glittered—a perfect grid of light and shadow. Somewhere out there, Liam sat behind glass and steel, a ghost in the system. Somewhere, a Bronze woman held her child close, knowing tomorrow would be harder. And somewhere, Isaac worked in an office, eyes fixed on a horizon only he could see.

Choices, she thought.

The word floated up, fragile, then crumbled on her tongue.

She reached through the stillness to touch the outline of her brother, nothing but a memory pressed thin against the quiet.

Remorse waited at the edge, but she left it there—untouched.

Best to be careful. Mother is watching.

The screen refreshed. Another case. Another name. Eve straightened her spine, smoothed her sleeves, and began again. The machine demanded Balance. And she, Gold and gleaming, would provide it. Even if her hands trembled. Even if the glass felt suddenly, terribly thin.

***

The train back to Gold Sector hummed beneath Eve's feet, a river of light and steel flowing through the city's veins. The evening pressed itself against the windows, bruised purple and gold, and the carriage glowed with the gentle hush of filtered lamps. She sat alone, her status glinting on her wrist, the seat molding itself around her as if to cradle her in the illusion of safety.

Her mind would not be cradled. It wandered, restless, circling the memory of Liam—her brother, her shadow, her undoing. She saw again the way the Enforcers had come for him: the silent approach, the red zero flashing, the way he had not resisted, only looked tired as if the world had already taken everything from him but his bones.

"It was one mistake, Eve. One."

His words haunted her, curling in the air between the carriage's soft music and the distant, mechanical lull of the city.

She closed her eyes and remembered her own hands, efficient and cold, moving his file through the system. She had flagged the anomaly, followed the rules.

Too many eyes. What choice did I have?

Mother demanded balance, and she had provided it, even as her heart trembled. Now, Liam was gone—erased, unpersoned, a ghost in the circuitry. She had tried to swallow her grief as she had been taught. But it burned inside her, a coal that would not cool.

The train slid through the city, and Eve's gaze drifted to the glass partition. Beyond, in the other carriages, the lesser tiers huddled together, their faces hollowed by fatigue and resignation. She watched them as she had that morning, but now something had shifted. Where once she saw only failure, now she saw the weight of the world pressing down, relentless and unfair. The boy with his face pressed to the glass, his mother's hand tight around his wrist. Eve saw Liam's eyes in his, wide and hungry, afraid to hope.

Was it really a choice, she wondered now, or something written before birth?

"Climb or fall," she had whispered, but the words tasted false.

The system was a maze, and some were born at the center, others at the edges, always searching for a way in. Maybe it was not will or work that decided who rose and who was crushed, but something colder, more arbitrary—a flick of a switch, a missed entry, a single mistake.

The train slowed, lights flickering across the glass. Eve's reflection stared back at her: composed, immaculate, Gold Tier perfect. But beneath the surface, she felt the cracks spreading, the old certainty dissolving. She looked away, searching the carriage, and her breath caught.

She saw him. Again.

Isaac.

Three rows ahead, his profile sharp against the window, eyes fixed on the blur of city lights. He looked untouchable, distant, as if the world outside held secrets only he could see. The memory of their last encounter flickered through her: the awkwardness, the emptiness, the way he had ignored her wave that morning. Something in her chest twisted—anger, longing, the ache of wanting to be seen.

She stood, smoothed her skirt, and walked down the aisle, her steps silent on the soft flooring. She stopped beside his seat, waited until he turned. For a moment, he said nothing, only blinked as if surprised to find her there.

"Why did you ignore me this morning?" she asked calmly, containing her emotions.

Isaac's eyes widened, then dropped. "I didn't see you," he said, too quickly. "I was . . . distracted. Looking at something else, I suppose."

She studied him, searching for a crack in his composure. "That's not true," she said with a smile. Better a smile than a frown. "You saw me. You just didn't want to."

He hesitated, then nodded, the smallest motion. "I'm sorry, Eve. I didn't know what to say. After . . . our time together. After what Mother wanted."

Eve felt some tension holding within her shoulders, but quickly replaced with something softer, more uncertain. "It wasn't what I expected," she admitted. "I thought it would mean something. What we did. But it didn't. Not really. I wanted it to."

Isaac looked at her, his expression open, vulnerable. "Mother expects a lot from us. Sometimes, too much. I know it didn't work the way it was supposed to. But I'd like to try again. On our own terms. If you'll let me."

She hesitated, feeling the weight of the day, the ache of loss, the emptiness that had followed her since Liam's disappearance. She wanted to feel something—anything—other than the cold efficiency that ruled her life. She wanted to be touched, to be seen, to be more than a cog in the machine.

"Yes," she said, surprising herself with the certainty in her voice. "Come over tonight. Not for Mother. For us."

Isaac smiled, a real smile this time, small but genuine. "Thank you, Eve. I want that too."

The train slid into the Gold Sector station, the doors opening with a soft sigh. Eve stepped off, Isaac at her side, the city's lights spilling over them like a benediction. For a moment, the world felt softer, Mother's grip a little less tight. She glanced back at the train, at the faces pressed to the glass, the endless divisions of tier and fate.

Maybe climb or fall was a lie. Maybe the only real choice was to reach for another hand, even in the dark.

She took Isaac's, and together they walked into the night, the city humming quietly around them, the future unwritten and trembling with possibility.

3 BALANCE IS FEAR

THE APARTMENT WAS A HUSH of golden lamplight and city shadows. Outside, the world pressed flat against the glass, kept at bay by the soft hum of the air system—a mechanical lullaby. Eve paused in the entryway, Isaac beside her, both of them caught in the syrupy quiet. The city's lights blinked in the window. A thousand tiny eyes. Always watching. Always waiting.

"Do you ever feel them staring?" Eve whispered.

Isaac glanced at the window, his face pale in the amber glow. "Every night," he said. "Like they're waiting for us to slip."

Eve led him down the hallway, her footsteps muffled, the door to her bedroom sliding shut behind them with a sigh. She reached for him. Her hands trembling. Not with fear. But with a hunger that was part longing. Part defiance. Part the ache of being seen at last.

Isaac hesitated. His touch careful. Fingers hovering as if reading a manual only he could see. "Are you sure?" he asked.

She pressed closer, breath catching, fingers tracing the sharp line of his jaw. "I want to remember this," she said. "Just this. Not the rules. Not Mother. Not the city."

Their bodies met in the half-light, sheets cool and smooth beneath them. Isaac's skin was warm, heartbeat steady, and close. Eve closed her eyes and let the sensation wash over her—his hands on her waist, the press of his lips at her shoulder.

He whispered her name, uncertain, as if testing the sound. "Eve?"

She answered with a sigh, her voice strange and new in the dark. "Don't stop."

For a moment, the world shrank to this: heat of skin, the slow, uncertain rhythm of bodies learning each other, the fragile hope in the dark.

But memories crept in—Liam, her brother, her ghost, his absence cold at the edge of every heartbeat. The boy on the train, the woman weeping on the platform, faces behind the glass. All the rules she had followed. The files she had flagged. The lives she had measured and weighed.

She pressed her face to Isaac's chest, voice muffled. "Please, help me forget," she said.

Isaac's hands grew surer. His lips softer. His breath a hush at her ear. For a while, they moved together in the dark, city lights flickering across their skin, shadows tangled on the wall. It was not love. Not exactly. But it was something—something real, something alive, something that belonged to them and no one else.

Afterward, they lay side by side, silence thick with questions. Isaac stared at the ceiling, chest rising and falling in the soft light.

Eve traced circles on his arm, words tangled on her tongue. "Will you stay?" she asked, barely audible.

He sat up, swinging his legs over the edge of the bed, searching for his shirt in the dimness. "I don't know if I can."

Eve watched him dress, heart thudding with a new, unfamiliar fear. "Don't go. Not yet."

He paused in the doorway, backlit by the city's glow. "The world's waiting," he said. "But I wish it wasn't."

The hallway beyond was dark, the city's hum muffled and distant. Eve slipped out of bed, the sheet wrapped around her, and crossed to him. She took his hand, small and cold in hers, and looked up at him, searching his face for something she could not name.

"Isaac," she whispered. "Do you . . . do you love . . . me?"

He looked down at her. His eyes shadowed. Unreadable. For a moment, she thought he might lie. Might say the words she wanted to hear. But instead, he shook his head. Just once. Slow and sad.

"That would depend," he said softly, "on the results of our lovemaking. And on what Mother would want."

The words dropped between them, quiet and heavy, stirring the silence as if the air itself remembered how to shiver. Eve's breath paused, suspended in her throat, a single fragile note on the verge of breaking. Hope dimmed in her chest, not all at once, but in increments, as if a curtain were being drawn across a window at dusk.

She let go of his hand. Stepped back. The sheet slid from her shoulders, whispering down her arms, a hush in a room that had run out of things to say.

Isaac reached out as if to comfort her but stopped himself. He looked at her for a long moment, something like sorrow in his eyes. He then turned and slipped into the hallway, the door closing behind him with a sigh.

She drifted from the door, her feet soundless on the cold tile, the sheet trailing behind her like shed skin from a story already ending. The apartment felt cavernous now, echoing with what hadn't been said. She had pictured it: the turn of a knob, a figure in the doorway, a voice breaking the hush with anything—anything at all. But no sound came. Only a hush that grew thicker, deeper, settling in like old dust in corners long untouched. The walls seemed to lean inward, the ceiling lower somehow. The shadows edged closer. They knew. She stood in the stillness, her skin bare to the room, her lungs full of ache. And there, in the hush, her hope cracked, fine as frost on morning glass, and fell to the floor in pieces too small to gather.

"Does anyone ever listen back?" she said, her voice barely more than a thought sent drifting into the dark.

No answer but the distant sound of trains, slicing through the night. "There they go," she murmured, "carrying the weary, the hopeful, the forgotten. All of them home. Or somewhere that passes for home. What does it all matter."

She wandered to the window, pressing her forehead to the cold pane. The chill anchored her. Kept her from drifting too far into memory. Far below, the sector boundaries cut the city into neat geometry—Gold, Silver, Bronze.

"Cages," she said, tracing a line in the condensation. "Just cages with different names."

A memory flickered: the boy from the train, his breath fogging the glass, eyes wide with wanting.

"Is he asleep now?" she asked the city. "Is he dreaming of a world without glass?"

A siren wailed, then faded. The lullaby of the city. She closed her eyes, hearing Liam's laughter in the hush.

"Bet you can't make it past curfew," he'd said once, grinning in the dark.

"Bet you can't," she'd shot back, heart pounding as they slipped through the shadows.

"Where are you now, Liam?" she asked the empty room. "What does Mother do with those she erases? Are you dreaming? Do you remember me?"

She stepped back from the window, arms wrapped tight around herself. The ache inside her was sharp, not just for Liam or Isaac. But for the girl she'd been before the rules became bone. Before every feeling was measured and weighed.

"Can love really be a line in Mother's ledger?" she wondered aloud. "Can it be reduced to an outcome?"

A breeze stirred outside. For a moment, she closed her eyes and let herself believe it was the breath of another world. One where sorrow and longing and hope weren't weaknesses to be audited. But proof of being alive.

"Just for a heartbeat," she said, her voice soft, "let me imagine that world."

She turned from the window, letting the city's light fall behind her. The apartment was quiet, but not empty. She carried the memory of touch, the echo of Isaac's voice, the ghost of her brother's laughter.

"I'll carry you all," she promised the silence. "Through every corridor. Every audit. Every silent night. I'm not lost. Not yet."

***

Eve made tea in silence. In ritual. In hope. The cup breathed steam into the air like a ghost exhaling. She held it close. Let it touch her lips. It tasted like forgotten rooms and empty chairs. Rainwater steeped in longing.

A flicker tickled her wrist. The implant blinked to life, cold and cheerful.

+25 points: Procreation completed.

Tap.

-20 points: No pregnancy.

Still Gold. Still polished. Still pristine.

The city outside hummed like a lullaby played too many times. Nothing cracked. Nothing changed. The walls held. The system yawned and carried on, unimpressed by the small tremors of a human heart.

She remembered Finn.

That quiet boy. Limbs like twigs. Eyes like shutters never quite open. Zero Tier. Already fading before the Enforcers came. No screams. No questions. He'd turned like a ghost remembering its shape. She watched. Couldn't help it. He passed into the state's arms like a page into a shredder. Then he was gone.

She never saw him again. Only heard the silence where he used to be.

Eve hadn't said a word then. Not to her teachers. Not to her parents. Not to anyone.

Liam, where are you? she thought.

She reached for her screen. The glow of it lit her face. She searched. Housing records. Department logs. Personal contacts. Liam's name didn't flicker. Didn't so much as blink.

It was as if he'd never drawn breath.

The apartment dulled around her. She turned the volume down on her apartment's speaker system and let the silence settle in. Outside, the false sky curled from corporate blue to a synthetic dusk, painted by algorithms and rules. The news played on a loop behind her. But she didn't listen. The same slogans echoed: Mother Sees All, Balance Is Peace, Your Points Are Your Life.

Her mind, stubborn and slow, inched back. Back to Liam's voice. That last thread of him.

"It was one mistake."

But Mother left no space for mistakes. She did not forget, and she certainly did not pardon. That was lesson one, hour one. Forgiveness was a virus. Forgiveness was a sickness of the soul. A flaw. And she had written the cure in bright, ruthless lines of code. The algorithm was precise, sharp as a scalpel, and just as cold. She created the system for a Class 3 Anomaly. Defined it. Created the consequences. Had drawn the lines that erased him.

And now Liam was gone.

Eve stared at her tea until it went cold. Then she reached for her screen again.

She didn't know what she was looking for. Not exactly. But her fingers hovered over her own record. She knew the risk. To open one's own logs was to invite scrutiny. Every query was tracked.

Still, she keyed it in. Her name. Her history. Her rise from Bronze to Gold. All clean. No infractions. No doubts.

And yet.

In the silence, she whispered the words she hadn't dared say in fifteen years. Words she'd buried when Finn was taken. Words she'd tried to forget when Liam said the system was broken.

"It's not balance," she said softly. "It's fear."

And once spoken, the words did not go away. They sat there in the quiet. Stubborn. Unwelcome. A bruise beneath the skin that would not fade.

Stop, she told herself. Move gently now. Mind the corners. Mother sees more than she lets on. She reads the tremble in a breath, the heat behind the eyes.

She turned off the lights and sat in the dark.

Tomorrow, she would go to work. She would smile. She would sip her tea. Do her work. Not say his name.

But tonight, she remembered. And she did not forgive.

***

It did not begin with sirens. Nor with the shriek of metal. Or the blue-white spit of a dying screen. No. It began with something smaller. A flicker. Human. Not electric. The sort of thing that slips in on cat paws while you're brushing your teeth, or folding towels, or standing in the hush between seconds. A breath caught sideways. A question that didn't want to be asked. The flutter of a moth's wing behind the eyes.

Eve noticed it first on a Tuesday, that most ordinary of days, pressed from the mold and set out to dry. The sky was a slab of blue, clouds arranged like furniture in a waiting room. Her apartment, all in the approved shades of calm, reflected the light just so.

The cup of tea in her hand chirped, digital and bright.

+2 points for healthy beverage selection.

It made her smile, barely. The shower had given her +5 for water efficiency minutes before. The system purred, content, a cat too sleek to bother with the chase.

"All is well," she murmured. But her words fell flat.

Except her brother was gone.

They had come for him. Enforcers. Black and polished. Their footsteps too soft. The hush of their presence like cold air leaking under a door. They pointed to the red zero pulsing on his wrist, silent as a fire alarm with no sound. That was all it took. No words. No shouts. Just silence—the kind that settles when someone leaves and takes the center of the room with them.

She remembered the moment. "This is all counterproductive," she whispered as if the walls might answer back.

Eve tried, as she had with every passing hour, to tuck the memory of Liam into some quiet corner—his laugh like sunlight through blinds, the echo of his shape in every hallway, the way his not-being there pushed gently, insistently, at the edges of her thoughts.

Don't think of him, she told herself. Don't think of Isaac either. Don't think of the others."

Work was what mattered. The neat rows of data. The glowing screens. The points she could still earn. She pressed her thoughts into order, folding them as tightly as towels. But Liam's absence fluttered at the corners of her mind.

Now she sat at the table. Her spoon tracing slow orbits in her cereal. Round and round. As if sketching the lonely rings of a world long gone cold. The cereal cooled, flavorless. Her lens blinked.

"-3 points. Late for work," the voice in her ear said.

She stood. Not with rage. Not with grief. But with the hollow motion of a machine resetting itself.

"All is well," she said, and the room said nothing back.

***

The Data Ethics Hub gleamed with a cold, child's-dream sheen. Smooth as poured milk. Bright as a promise. Humming with the secret music of circuits. The air smelled of ozone and something sharper, the scent of order enforced. Analysts perched in their tier-colored chairs. Neat as petals in a garden no wind could touch. Fingers dancing over keys in a silent ballet. Above, the lights pulsed slow and thoughtful, like the heartbeat of a machine that dreamed.

Eve hesitated, her question a stone in her mouth. She had sworn—today, she would not look back. She would fold her thoughts, tuck away the ache, let Liam's name dissolve in the hum of the system. But the silence pressed at her. Insistent. Until she felt herself moving, compelled by a force she could not name.

Sarci glided over, his smile lacquered and stiff, the platinum flicker of his wrist implant catching every stray light. He looked like something built for display. A mannequin with a pulse. A grin painted on just so.

"You look like a minus-five day," he said, his lips curving but his eyes flat and empty, as if he'd never seen a real sorrow.

Eve's own smile didn't come. Her voice, when it emerged, was softer than she meant. A whisper wrapped in velvet. Almost afraid of itself.

"Did you see Liam's audit report?" Eve asked. Her voice crackled with something. Sadness. Deep sadness. "The one they posted?"

Sarci shrugged, his movement too smooth to be sincere. "I make a habit of not chasing ghosts, Eve. Ghosts are zeroes. And zeroes are contagion."

Eve didn't answer. She only tapped open the screenview, the glow blooming like a dangerous flower in the dark. Mother's hallmark: sky blues, nursery pinks—colors that used to mean lullabies and soft blankets, but here they meant razors. Razors beneath ribbons.

She typed in Liam's ID.

The display blinked cold.

ACCESS DENIED.

She tried again. Slower this time, as if typing with her breath. One keystroke. Another.

DENIED.

Sarci leaned closer, and when he spoke, his words came dressed in velvet, but you could hear the hinge of a guillotine just behind each syllable.

"Look, you got points to burn, but not enough for that question. You want to stay Gold? You forget him."

But Sarci—he saw it. The flicker, the ache just behind her eyes. The way her throat caught, like a note played on broken strings. He felt it in a place he rarely let feel. Something brushed the edge of his polished language, a memory, maybe, or just an echo of what it meant to still carry love for the dead.

He stepped back, just a fraction. Enough.

She stared at the screen. Eyes unmoving. Her reflection shimmered on the soft pink screen like a ghost drawn in steam— there, and then not.

"He's my brother."

Sarci didn't blink.

"He was your brother. Mother knows best."

Her hand twitched. A flicker sparked behind her eyes, the kind that starts fires.

***

In the lunch area, her food arrived like a ritual, wrapped in quiet murmurs and the soft shuffle of shoes against antiseptic tile. The conversation was measured, approved. Smiles were practiced things. No one mentioned the division by tier—why bother naming gravity or air? Eve sat where Golds were meant to sit. On a bench, the color of prosperity. Her sandwich wrapped in glossy cellofilm stamped with Mother's wisdom: Every good deed strengthens the hive.

She stared at it. Bread. A slab of protein paste. A slogan stamped across it in edible ink like a smile that didn't quite reach the eyes. Then something flickered behind her gaze—an old ember. She set it down beside her and rose, silent as a thought taking shape.

She slipped from the lunch area, her credentials guiding her past the locked gates of routine. Downward she went, into the hushed underlayers of the building, where the air moved differently as if remembering an older time. The walls here breathed slow. Pipes ticked. Lights hummed their own quiet songs. It was closer to the bones of things, where the structure forgot its mask.

The corridors stretched out, empty as dreamless sleep. She found what she needed—an unattended maintenance room with dust in the corners and the smell of old electricity. She eased into the chair at the console. Fingers moving with memory, not thought. A line of code. A bypass. A quiet override. No way to trace her. The panel blinked once. Blinked again. Then agreed.

Liam had shown her the trick, not out of rebellion, not quite. It was a gift wrapped in curiosity, given on a slow afternoon when the building sighed with heat and the lights flickered as if dreaming. He had leaned in close, voice low, not secretive but sacred, like someone recounting how the stars once spoke in Morse.

"This is how you listen," he'd said, tapping the console not like a machine, but like an old friend. "The building speaks, if you know the rhythms. If you treat it gentle."

He hadn't taught her to break things. Just to look for things. Things hidden. Forgotten scripts left behind like footprints. Permissions left cracked like old paint. He showed her how to press without bruising, to lean into the system like a door that might open if you only knew where the hinge was softest.

Now, alone in the hush of the maintenance room, she rerouted a proxy node, her fingers dancing across the keys with the same quiet confidence Liam once had. She accessed the deletion queue, where things went to vanish, but not all the way. There was a shadow log—always a shadow log—and she opened it like a book no one else remembered how to read. She entered a bypass string, one Liam had made her memorize syllable by syllable, like a lullaby in code. She set a loop. Hid her edits beneath decoy commands. The console flickered, paused, and accepted her instructions like an old friend remembering her name.

This wasn't force. It was finesse. A question posed so carefully the system didn't know it was answering.

Then it happened.

There he was.

Liam.

Folded into the list like a misfiled dream.

Zero Tier: Unauthorized Inquiry.

Her fingers trembled over the keys. Not with fear. But with something older. A flicker of rage or grief or both. Stitched tight in her chest. She followed the digital trail like a path through darkened woods. Breadcrumb by breadcrumb. His logs pulsed back at her, whispering truths in code. He had not failed. He had asked. He had seen. Deep dives into the shimmering Platinum core of power. Into the metrics of the untouchable. But what she saw was wrong. The numbers were off. Too high. Much too high. Even for Platinum.

The logs ended three days before his arrest. Three days. That was how long he had danced with truth before the silence swallowed him whole.

What was he doing?

***

After work, in the darkness of night, Eve drifted to the edge of the Gold Sector. It was a place where the gardens gave off their plastic perfume and the silver fountains sprayed recycled joy in arcs that glittered like laughter with no soul. There, just beyond the tidy hedges and harmony chimes, stood the boundary. And beyond that—Silver. She used to pity them. Those slumped figures in recycled denim and work-creased faces. Now she envied them. They lived closer to the truth. Raw and unperfumed.

A name flashed in her mind like an old tune on a dusty record: Cass. Liam's friend. A girl with a crooked smile and a voice like flint striking stone.

Eve hopped the rail. Her wrist buzzed.

50-point deduction. Leaving Gold Sector.

The air smelled different here. Heavier. Acrid.

The streets were calm in that way that never meant peace— just the absence of motion. Few people about, and those who were moved like shadows in the corners of things, their coats tight around them, heads down, eyes darting. Windows stared back, dim and silent. Streetlamps hummed but didn't shine right. It was the kind of quiet that felt borrowed, like someone had turned the volume down on a city that hadn't agreed to it.

She remembered the building. Found the door. She didn't knock. Just opened it.

Cass's flat was a capsule of forbidden things. The walls peeled with contraband flyers, their corners curling like they wanted to run. Hacked AR tags blinked slogans in angry neon— "Mother Lied" and "Your Points Are Chains." A rusted fan on the ceiling spun out a lazy rhythm, stirring the scent of ozone and melted plastic. The light in the room was sickly pink, filtered through a cracked windowpane and the eternal burn of a protest sign stuck to the wall with electrical tape and stubborn hope.

It smelled like memory and static. Somewhere you weren't supposed to be.

Cass saw her and didn't flinch. Didn't reach for anything sharp or silent. That counted.

"You've got guts, Gold," she said, voice like sand through wire. "What are you looking for?"

"My brother," Eve said. "Why he vanished."

Cass's laugh was brittle, broken at the edges. "Because he cared. That was his sin. Thought he could change the game from inside the casino. Fool heart, royal flush of dreams."

Eve stepped in farther. Told Cass about the logs. The missing audit. Numbers that seemed wrong. Out-of-place.

Cass leaned in like a match nearing paper. "He found them. Platinum-tier fraud. Score rigging. Value laundering without Mother knowing. They twist the system like old-world bookies. They do it quiet, clean. Mother doesn't even blink. Doesn't know. Your brother was going to out them. Show the wires. Pull the mask off the whole machine. Blow it wide open."

"And then he disappeared."

Cass nodded. The moment hung like a breath before a scream.

"And now you," she said, her voice lighter now, brittle as cellophane. "Gold-sector sweetheart with clean hands and glass shoes, dropped into the burn zone. So what's it going to be? You skip back to your virtue tower, slurp your compliance smoothies, and tuck yourself in under a blanket of lies? Or do we break the Queen? Topple the whole game and watch the pieces run?"

Eve stared. Her heart thumped like it wanted to run before she did. She could still see it in her mind—those falsified ledgers, the numbers with too many zeroes, the Platinum names highlighted not in red but in silence. She knew it was wrong. Knew they were rigging the very breath they breathed. And Mother—she wasn't watching. Or worse, didn't care.

"I don't know," Eve said. Her voice felt thin. "I don't know what to do. Where to start."

Cass grinned then. Sharp. A moon-slice smile. "I'd start by running."

***

Eve walked home through streets that whispered, the silence thick as velvet drawn over the world. Lamps hummed like forgotten lullabies. But even they dared not speak her name. She knew now. Knew what one was not meant to know. And somewhere in the towers above, behind invisible glass and humming servers, Mother knew she knew.

At her doorstep, the implant in her wrist blinked. Once. Twice. Ten settled into a soft red glow.

15-point deduction. Time spent in lesser sector.

The flicker in her chest caught. And became flame.

4 CRACKS IN THE SYSTEM

EVE AWOKE TO THE SOFT, persistent hum of the city—a sound that had once comforted her, a lullaby of order and efficiency. Now, it pressed in, a reminder of the invisible latticework that held every life in place. She lay still, eyes tracing the faint blue glow of her wrist implant as it pulsed with her current point total: 8,248. Gold Tier. Safe.

But safety was a fragile thing. She knew that now.

She dressed in silence, the fabric of her clothing smooth as still water, its faint shimmer like light caught in a pearl—regulation-approved, algorithm-certified, sterile in its beauty. Around her, the apartment did what it always did: obeyed. The walls hummed faintly with Mother's breath, embedded sensors tracking temperature, posture, heart rate. Furniture shifted subtly when she moved, angles recalibrated for optimal spine health. The air was scrubbed to the molecule, carrying the faint scent of lemon and compliance.

Each morning, the windows awoke before she did—gradient-glass panels that deepened or brightened depending on what Mother deemed most psychologically beneficial. The sun entered only in measurements, lux-calibrated, emotionally balanced, not a single ray out of order. Screens in the walls blinked softly behind paint-tones, waiting for her eye contact to spring to life with newsfeeds tailored by score, curated by virtue.

Mother's voice, never spoken but always there, made sure nothing fell into disarray. Even dust was forbidden. Even silence had its limits. The apartment was a sanctum of precision, a cathedral to surveillance.

Then, somewhere far below, a siren rose—brief, sharp, and distant. A cry in a world that no longer cried. Eve flinched. Not at the sound, but at the crack it carved in her carefully metered calm.

A memory came to her. Finn. The way his eyes had pleaded as he was led away. She remembered the teacher's smile. The way the lesson had resumed as if nothing had happened. She remembered the mantra: Mother knows best. She always does.

But now, with Liam gone, the words rang hollow.

Eve's commute was a procession of quiet perfection. The city's arteries flowed with citizens, each one marked by the subtle glow of their wrist implants. Enforcers glided through the crowds. Faceless and silent. Their visors reflecting the world in cold blue. Eve kept her head down. Her steps measured. Her expression neutral.

Inside the data center, the air was cool and dry, tinged with the scent of ozone. Holographic displays hovered above rows of workstations, each one a window into Mother's mind. Eve's station greeted her with a gentle chime: "Good morning, Eve. Your productivity yesterday was exemplary. +15 points."

She forced a smile. "Thank you, Mother."

Her coworker Sarci appeared at her elbow, immaculate as always. His suit was pressed to perfection, his hair a study in order.

He smiled, but his eyes flickered with something else—anxiety, perhaps, or calculation.

"Rough morning?" he asked, voice low.

Eve hesitated. "Just . . . tired."

Sarci nodded, glancing around. "About your brother. I'm sorry."

Eve's heart lurched. "Thank you. I appreciate that."

"You should be careful, Eve," He leaned in, voice barely above a whisper. "People are watching. Mother is watching."

She bristled. "But I haven't done anything wrong."

Sarci's smile tightened. "That's not always enough. You know that. I know you want to know more. About what happened. But don't dig. Just . . . focus on your work. Let the past go. It's safer that way."

Eve watched him walk away, his steps precise, his back rigid. She turned to her console, hands trembling. The screen came to life, lines of code cascading like rain.

She called up what she could on Liam. Nothing new. His transaction logged as a "Category 3 Infraction: Failure to Report Error." The data was clean—too clean. No timestamp. No supporting documentation. Just a single line. Final. Absolute. She checked the backup archives. A place where she hadn't been. Nothing. Empty.

A chill crept up her spine. Data didn't just vanish. Not in Mother's world.

A message blinked on her screen:

Unauthorized access detected. Please return to approved tasks.

Eve closed the file. Heart pounding. She glanced around. No one seemed to notice.

But someone always noticed.

She drifted through the day as though underwater, each moment muffled, each sound a distant chime in a submerged cathedral. Faces passed her in the corridors like ghosts too shy to speak. Words were spoken, but their meanings slid off her mind like water off glass. Somewhere, behind her eyes, a reel of memory played: glances exchanged, voices lowered, doors half-shut.

Then—like a candle stuttering in a forgotten attic—she remembered.

It had been months ago. Before the silence. Before the Enforcers came. Before the light in Liam's voice grew thin and flickered out. A message. One message.

Her hands moved without thought, coaxing a viewscreen awake. It flared gently, like a firefly in the dusk. She moved through the archive, finger gliding over the surface as if brushing dust from old books on a high shelf. There—quiet and small and waiting—was the message. Liam's. A voice from the past, preserved in pixels. Her heart skipped, then beat louder, as though it too remembered.

"Eve, if anything happens to me, look in the cracks. The system isn't as perfect as they want you to believe."

She hadn't understood then. She did now.

That night, Eve returned home, the city's lights a constellation of surveillance. She drew the curtains, checked the locks, and activated her privacy shield—a Gold Tier privilege, though she knew it was more illusion than protection.

She tried to think of all of Liam's friends, summoning their names like ghosts from a half-forgotten childhood—faces flickering across her mind's attic, dusty with time and silence. Not just Cass. Surely there had been others, hadn't there? Someone who had laughed with Liam beneath the streetlamps or shared whispers behind the walls lined with surveillance vines. She called up their names on her viewscreen, one by one. Each dissolved into polite refusals, stony silences, or nothing at all—vanished, like birds who'd flown south to escape the frost of suspicion. Their point totals glimmered like shields. Safety, bought in distance.

All but one.

Dante.

The name clung to the screen like breath on glass. Silver Tier.

She hesitated, then sent a message:

"Dante, it's Eve. I need to talk to you about Liam. Please."

The reply came minutes later, each word unfolding on the screen like a breath held too long:

"Not safe. Meet at the old transit hub. Midnight. Come alone."

And then, just as swiftly as it had arrived, the message unraveled—character by character, blinking out like dying stars until the screen was blank again.

Eve stared at the emptiness, pulse quickening. A shadow of code, a vanishing act. He must have something, she thought. Some hidden script, a cloaked program that dances past Mother's eyes like a whisper in fog.

Her pulse quickened. She knew the risks. Unauthorized movement after curfew was a minus 50-point infraction. But she had to know.

She waited as the city's curfew chime swept over the rooftops like the slow toll of a cathedral bell in a dying world. It echoed through concrete canyons and along glass facades, a sound both holy and hollow as if the city were praying and forgetting all at once. When silence followed, thick and knowing, she stepped into it like a swimmer into cold water.

The alleys swallowed her. They were veins of darkness stitched between the glowing organs of the city, places where the rules thinned and the shadows told stories older than Mother. Her wrist implant, once bright as a starling's breast, now flickered low and dim—just a heartbeat in hiding.

At night, the city exhaled its truths. Even in the Gold Sector. The perfect symmetry of daylight unraveled, corners grew teeth, and the neon dreams of Mother blurred into ghostlight. Eve moved with careful breath, feeling watched even where there were no eyes. Somewhere, a distant drone purred, mechanical and uncaring.

She found the old transit hub not by directions, but by the buried thread of memory that tugged her through the empty avenues. It hunched between towers like a fossilized creature, spine bowed beneath its shattered glass shell, the roof patchworked with old rains and spidered fractures. Pigeons dreamed above in the rusted girders, wings twitching in sleep. The air here held the scent of iron filings and cinders and years too stubborn to pass.

Dante stood there, carved from shadow, a silhouette the dark had spared. He had crossed from the Silver Sector, leaving safety behind like a coat on a hook. The lines on his face told stories—no sleep, too much truth. He didn't move toward her. He didn't have to. The night already had.

"You shouldn't have come," he said, and the words came slow and hoarse as if the truth had cost him breath.

"I need to know what happened to Liam," she said.

His eyes flashed with something—a warning, a kindness, a wound. Then he nodded, almost to himself.

"He was getting close," Dante said. "Too close. He dipped his fingers in the Platinum Tier and came up with dirt. Corruption. Point manipulation. He thought if he could show the truth, the system would heal."

Eve's lungs caught and held the air. "Did he tell anyone?" she asked, but already she knew the answer. It was in the way Dante looked away, like he was searching the dark for a voice that had already gone silent.

"He tried," Dante said, and his voice felt like wind blowing over a grave. "But Mother's always listening. Platinum Tier—they don't just erase points, Eve. They erase existence."

The words echoed like footsteps in an empty hall. Eve drew her arms around herself as if to hold her shape in place. "I saw the numbers. They were wrong. Very wrong. But why did he get involved in all this?" she asked, though the question came out soft, like a child asking the dark to be kind.

Dante watched her with the haunted patience of someone who'd seen too many veils yanked from the world, too many ugly truths wriggling in the light. "Because he knew," he said softly, "what the rest of us only whisper to ourselves in sleepless hours. That all this"—he gestured at the city, the skyline, the glittering carcass of civilization—"is a stage built on lies. Liam saw the nails in the beams, the rust in the screws. He had that kind of heart—honest, stubborn, lit up like dry kindling."

A breath passed. "But fire like that?" Dante said, voice low. "It draws eyes. And eyes mean trouble."

"You speak like he's dead," Eve said.

Dante paused, as if the silence itself might contradict him. "You dig far enough, you don't just find secrets. You fall into them. And when you do, you don't leave footprints."

Eve didn't flinch. Her voice was firm, clenched like a fist behind the ribs. "I don't believe he's gone."

She let the words hang, suspended like smoke.

"I have to know. I have to try."

He sighed—a sound like old hinges giving way. "Then you'll need more than courage. There's a group. The Nulls. Ghosts that walk without light. People who've been rubbed out, or begged to be. They're the only ones still dreaming."

"Where?" she asked.

Dante shook his head. "They find you. If they think you're worth the risk."

And then, as if from some long-forgotten storybook, he placed an object in her hand. A relic. A whisper. A key. A data chip. Worn smooth in places. Nicked. Scuffed like it had spent years rattling in the pocket of a man chased by machines.

"Liam said you'd know what to do with this," Dante murmured.

She closed her fingers around it, and it felt like closing a door behind her. "Thank you," she whispered, though he was already folding back into the shadows, dissolving into the ruins like steam into sky.

Eve walked home beneath the electric stars of the city, her thoughts spinning like the wheels of an old watch winding down. Drones passed overhead, blinking red. Cameras followed her like silver insects. But her pace didn't change.

Inside her apartment, where everything still pretended to be safe, she slid the chip into her console. The screen blinked once. Then again. And then the truth poured out, line by glowing line. All the names. All the numbers. All the dates. And all the lies.

At the top of the list:

Platinum Tier Overrides—Confidential.

Eve leaned in, her face bathed in the pale light of treason. She scrolled. She scrolled. She scrolled. Each entry like a crack running through stained glass. Names she knew—executives with practiced smiles, politicians with polished palms. Even Sarci. Points lifted. Penalties deleted. Lives rewritten.

Then—Liam.

His name. The red flag beside it.

Under investigation.

No details. Just silence.

At the bottom, a message blinked in ghostly white:

"If you're reading this, you know the truth. Don't trust anyone. Not even yourself."

Eve stared. And something ancient in her bones—something iron-bound and fire-fed—rose like a storm off the sea.

Mother wasn't god. She was wire and voltage and voices in tin cans, built by men long ago who sweated fear and soldered lies. That lullaby, the one they piped into cribs and classrooms—Mother knows best—wasn't a comfort. It was a collar. A curse.

She shut the file with trembling fingers.

The city outside kept humming. Same as ever. The stars on the towers still blinked their synthetic rhythms. But Eve felt the shift in her bones. The fracture. The beginning of something else.

She would find the Nulls.

She would set fire to the lie.

Even if it meant vanishing into the dark herself.

Then came the notification.

Unauthorized movement after curfew.
Immediate 50-point deduction.
Gold Tier. Stable.
Explanation may be required.

                    ***

The next day at work, the city moved around Eve like a great mechanical beast, humming and sighing and blinking its thousand blinking eyes. And Eve—Eve moved through it like a shadow without weight, her limbs remembering how to walk among the living while her mind wandered among the vanished. Sarci's glance flicked past her like a scanning beam—clinical, brief, uncaring—and she returned it with the precision of a machine half-remembering its purpose. Her words were trimmed to bone, brittle leaves spoken in frost.

Enforcers drifted by like memories borrowed from someone else's fever dream—silent, seamless, born from mist and alloy beneath the sugar-blue hush of morning. They didn't walk; they floated, like whispers in chrome, thought-forms behind mirrored masks, their presence folding into the city's sigh. Eve used to drop her gaze, match her heartbeat to the rhythm of obedience, swallow dread like a hard little stone. But not now. Now she stared straight through them, wide-eyed and awake, as if a pane of glass she'd lived behind had finally thinned. The lie had split— hairline, delicate—and through that slender break, something unseen shifted. She wondered if they would pause, turn, speak. Ask where she'd wandered while the curfew sang its silver lull. Wondered if they already knew. Or if knowing had ever really mattered.

At noon, the break room shone with sterilized light and the scent of synthetic coffee. Sarci appeared beside her like a magician's trick, conjured from chrome and routine. His teeth showed, but they weren't smiling.

"You seem distracted," he said, the words polished smooth as plastic.

"Just not feeling well," she answered, the lie sliding easily from her lips. She wondered if it was still a lie.

"Go see a Med," he told her. Then he leaned in as if sharing a secret, but his voice carried the cold of steel. "Remember what we talked about? You're not planning anything . . . reckless, are you?"

She turned her gaze on him, long and slow, searching for the old Sarci who used to laugh at lunchtime, who once gave her half a muffin and didn't ask for anything back. He was gone. Or maybe he'd never been.

"Of course not."

He seemed pleased by that. "Good. If you continue to work hard. Follow the rules. You can be Platinum. Remember, Eve—Mother sees everything."

She nodded because that was what was expected. "I know," she said. "Bless her."

But her affirmation was hollow. There was no soul behind it. Inside, something had lifted. Like a window stuck for years now open, letting in air that smelled of rust and rebellion. There was no fear. None.

I will find them, she thought. The Nulls.

That night, she knew where her feet must carry her. The city breathed below her like some vast dreaming creature wrapped in wires and whispers, its breath warm with ozone beneath the hard sheen of artificial stars. In the distance, the curfew sirens cried their thin metal lullaby, and Eve slipped between alley shadows like a smudged note on the edge of a burned-out record.

She reached the old transit hub. Its ribs still held the shape of purpose, even as mold crept along the girders and vines of cable sagged from above like tired memories. The place smelled of rust, dust, and the ghost of momentum. Shattered glass lay in patterns like constellations scattered by a careless god. The benches, warped and weary, remembered better days.

Time stretched thin. She waited, heartbeat tangled with the silence. Minutes swam past her like leaves on dark water.

Maybe I was wrong to come here, she thought.

And just as she was about to give up—turn back, vanish into the hum of her obedient apartment—something moved.

A figure came from the dark. A woman carved from grit and fire. Muscles like ropes. Scars like stories. Her voice was a flint spark in the gloom.

"You're Eve."

"Yes."

She gave a single nod, the kind that didn't ask questions because it already knew the answers. "I'm Zara. Dante said your name like it mattered. Said you could be counted on. Said you're Liam's sister."

Something struck like a bell inside Eve. "Are you—?"

"What?" Zara's tone didn't rise. It crouched.

"The Nulls?"

"I'm one of a tide. And the tide's coming."

"How did you know I'd be here?"

"Didn't. Just felt it. A ripple through the wires. A sister's love tugging the world toward a crack in the code. That kind of thing leaves a mark. You want to fight? Show me."

And Eve did not flinch. Not anymore. The fear was there, yes, but it no longer ran the show. "Tell me what to do."

Zara smiled then. Not kindly. It was the kind of smile a knife might wear. Gleaming at the edge of a breath. "First, you survive. Then, you learn."

They walked together through the city's veins—beneath the ordered layers of Mother's world. Places she didn't know existed. Where the wires grew wild and the silence whispered things too old to forget. The tunnels smelled of rust and damp, but they were alive. Down here, people lived outside Mother's grasp, outside the script. Down here, ghosts walked with names and eyes that still remembered light.

Others watched as she passed. Some nodded. Some looked away. Each face held its own story: grief etched in tired lines, hope hidden behind a blink. No one spoke. They didn't need to.

Zara stopped at a door that looked like it had grown from the wall itself. She pressed her palm to a scanner, and the door sighed open, slow and reluctant. Inside, screens blinked with uneven breath. Lights flickered like candle ghosts.

"This is our world," Zara said. "No points. No ranks. Just people."

Eve stepped forward as if entering a half-remembered dream, spun from copper wires and breathless hush. The room, dimly lit by scavenged bulbs that pulsed like tired fireflies, swam with the scent of rust and memory. Dante stood there, his eyes hollow lanterns lit by things he could never unsee.

And beside him stood others—Rei and Sana—like memories caught in a summer wind, drifting in from some half-remembered dream. They were young. The world had once danced for girls like them. Rei with her dusk-colored eyes and hair that curled like the end of a question, Sana with laughter still tucked behind her lips, her beauty like sunlight through rain. They stood bathed in the golden hush of memory, radiant and unreachable, their faces written not in sorrow, but in the soft, aching script of things once held and lost.

Zara's voice broke the stillness, low and steady as a heart refusing to stop. "We're what remains," she said, not with sorrow, but steel. "Mother wants silence. Erasure. But we remember. And we remain."

Eve's voice trembled out of her. "How? How do you stay alive?"

Zara's lips curled into a tired smile. "We float just beneath the surface, where the machines don't stir. We let our numbers glow just enough. No more. No less. Safe enough to be ignored."

"And then?" Eve asked, the words like smoke in the air.

"And then we vanish," Zara said. "At night, we slip between cracks in the world. Tunnels older than Mother. Ducts and passages lined with dust and forgetting. The city forgets, you see. It forgets its bones. But we don't."

"Are there passages near where I live?"

Zara gave a slow nod and passed her a worn map, soft at the folds. "Yes. This will show you."

Eve's voice was quiet, but it rang like iron. "I want to help."

Zara studied her the way one studies a flame—curious if it will flicker or grow. Then she handed her a tablet.

"Start by learning the system. If you want to fight Mother, you need to learn how she dreams."

Eve took it, the tablet warm from another's hands. Her fingers curled around it like it was a key.

She would learn. She would fight. For Liam's vanished voice. For Finn's empty chair. For the cold places where names used to be. And this time, she would not look away.

Later that night, Eve followed the map, its lines drawn in hurried ink, like veins on the back of an old hand. She made her way to her apartment by way of the forgotten veins of the city— the tunnels beneath the earth that once pulsed with the lifeblood of a more human time. The walls were slick with condensation and time itself, smelling faintly of rust, machine oil, and something older still—coal dust, maybe, or memory. Her footsteps echoed through the catacombs, lonely and defiant, swallowed quickly by the hush of ancient concrete and humming wires. Shadows danced against the pipework as if remembering the ones who had walked this route before her—workers, rebels, ghosts of a vanished world.

She came upon the ancient ladder, its rungs polished soft from the touch of countless careful fingers, and climbed steadily into the heart of her block. Through the hidden panel behind the utility cabinet, she slipped, as if stepping through a veil into a quiet new life. A few twisting halls later, her apartment opened before her, wrapped in a hush that seemed to hold its breath. Not the sterile quiet the system demanded, but the hush of a place holding its breath.

The lights came on without being asked. The air adjusted to a familiar temperature. The windows dimmed, filtering out the city's neon arteries. And as the door slid shut behind her with a sigh, she looked down at her wrist.

The implant glowed soft blue, a tiny lighthouse against her skin. She held it up, heart tapping out a question in her ribs.

No notifications.

No deductions.

No reprimands from the ever-seeing, ever-knowing eyes.

She exhaled slowly and sat on the edge of her bed, half-expecting some automated voice to spill from the ceiling, warm and maternal. Nothing came.

She was still safe. For now.

***

Steam rose, curling and twisting, painting the glass with a soft, milky haze. Eve stood at the edge of the tiles, her reflection wavering—sharp cheekbones, dark eyes, hair twisted in a knot that had survived another day in the machinery of order.

She peeled away her clothes, the fabric whispering secrets. "Another day, another mask," she murmured, folding each piece with the same care she gave her thoughts.

Her eyes met their own reflection in the glass. "You look like trouble," she whispered, lips curving. "Or maybe just a question no one wants to answer." The mirror offered no reply, only the shimmer of danger in her eyes—beautiful, yes, but the beauty of a blade.

She stepped into the shower. The water roared hot, searing her skin like a flame unbridled. She stood still. "Go on," she said to the streaming heat. "Do your worst."

The city's hum faded, replaced by the steady drumbeat of water, the hush and sigh of steam. She closed her eyes. Drifted.

A name surfaced. The Nulls. She heard it in Dante's voice—soft, urgent, forbidden. "Ghosts that walk without light," he'd said. "People who've been rubbed out, or begged to be. They're the only ones still dreaming."

She had crossed a line for them.

"Am I marked now?" she asked the steam, tracing invisible scars. "Would you know it if you saw me, Liam?"

She pictured her brother's face: stubborn jaw, laughter that filled rooms. "Did you know I'd follow?" she asked the empty air. "Were you afraid?"

The water traced her skin, washing away sweat and fear, but not the questions. She remembered the points—those numbers glowing on every wrist.

"Just code," she muttered. "Just numbers. But they decide everything."

She'd seen the files, the Platinum Tier overrides, the way lives were rewritten with a keystroke. "How does Mother see everything and nothing?" she wondered aloud. "How does rot grow in a perfect garden?"

She pressed her forehead to the cool tile. "If anything happens to me, look in the cracks," Liam's message echoed. "The system isn't perfect."

She let the words settle, heavy as water.

"What will I find in those cracks?" she asked. "Hope? Or just more darkness?"

She stayed until the water ran cold, until her skin was flushed and her mind finally quiet. She stepped out, wrapped herself in a towel, and faced the mirror again. Her eyes were darker now, deeper. "Still Eve," she said, voice low. "Still sharp. But not the same."

She dressed in silence, each movement deliberate. At the window, she looked out at the city—lights blinking in their measured rhythm, towers rising like the bones of some ancient beast.

"Somewhere out there, the Nulls wait," she said. "Somewhere, the truth. Maybe even you, Liam."

She touched the implant on her wrist, feeling the pulse of her point total. "Safe, for now," she said. "But safety's just another story they tell us." She turned from the window, her reflection fading into the dark, and began to plan, the night alive with questions.

***

Days unraveled. Not cleanly, not in threads, but like old reels of film left too long in heat—melting, sticking, spooling into something unrecognizable. Down in the tunnels, time didn't tick; it breathed. A slow exhale through rusted ducts and iron bones, warm with the breath of forgotten machines. The Nulls lived in that breath. They listened to it. Moved with it.

"Listen," Dante said one night, crouched beside a cracked pipe as condensation wept down the walls. His voice was low, meant for stone and wire, not air. "Up there, they live like nothing's watching. Down here, everything listens."

Eve placed her hand against the damp wall. A tremor passed through her fingertips—not mechanical, not quite human. "It's like the tunnels are dreaming."

Dante gave a nod, something close to a smile tugging at the edge of him. "More like remembering."

She stopped counting days the way people stop counting heartbeats—useless, endless, meaningless under all that weight of stone and silence. The surface had its clocks, its rituals, its sunsets, and bells. It had Mother. Down here, there was only breath and grit. Hard work. Once, she collapsed, her back pressed to the cold, dreaming in the space between seconds. Rei nudged her awake with the toe of a boot. No words. Just the world waiting.

She trained until her muscles howled like old machines begging for oil, then trained again. In the beginning, her steps rang out—sharp, uncertain, full of the self. Now they whispered, soft as dust, leaving nothing behind but air. She could drift through doorways like a breeze that never learned its name. Her breath grew thin and precise. Her questions, once wandering things, turned narrow and silver-edged, knives tucked behind her teeth.

During the day, she returned to her analyst's chair. Mother's code stretched before her in endless columns, a language she'd once feared. Now it read like a confession. Not just surveillance. Not just control. But decay. Hairline faults beneath the polished surface. Whole blocks of code behaving like they'd been patched too many times, too quickly, stitched together like borrowed skin.

"See that?" she muttered, tapping the screen. "It's not perfect. Not anymore."

Janel, a colleague, glanced over, eyes wary. "Careful, Eve. Mother hears more than you think."

She shrugged, lips tight. "Let her listen. Maybe she'll learn something."

And then the night came, the tunnels called, and she slipped into the underworld with Dante again. Their maps weren't maps. They were memories passed down in chalk and ink, thumbed edges, water-warped corners. Beneath the streets, they traced the ghost lines of data cables, stepping over the wreckage of systems too old to repair.

"Where's this all heading?" she asked, brushing her fingers along a sealed hatch.

"Forward," Dante grinned, "but it'll feel like falling backward. Trust me."

He showed her how to vanish—how to be absence instead of presence. How to wait. How to make a strike feel like a whisper.

She learned to read the weight in another's stance, the quiver before motion.

One night, she failed a drill, caught off-balance. He caught her.

"Pain's just tuition," he said, brushing the dust from her elbow. "You're already paying."

When she came back limping, Rei handed her a wet cloth, grinning. "Congratulations. You look like one of us now."

Sana just pressed a thermos into her hand. "Drink. You've burned through whatever was keeping you human."

Eve didn't laugh. The change had come quiet, gradual. Her movements sharper, her thoughts colder. She no longer looked toward the upper levels with longing. Gold Tier? The old apartment with its filtered sun? Just postcards from a lie.

"I don't miss it," she said one night, watching the city's distant glow through a storm grate above. "None of it. It's all just dust pretending to shine."

Dante touched her shoulder. "Then you're ready," he said. "Now you begin."

She was a Null. Belonged to the dark now. To the sparks of rebellion lit in the tunnels and alleys of a forgotten city.

One sleepless night, Liam's voice came to her. Over and over again.

"If you're reading this, you know the truth. Don't trust anyone. Not even yourself."

The words hit her like the wind before a storm. She didn't cry at first. Just lay there, staring at the ceiling, her fingers curled into fists. Then the tears came, hot and quick, vanishing almost as soon as they touched her cheeks. Grief had taught her to cry without sound.

As she stared at the ceiling, the room around her was small, quiet. But she began to hear sounds in her mind. The murmuring in code. Others passing tools to others, sharing information, code, and sketching plans. A new world being written one risk at a time.

Eve took a breath, deep and deliberate. Liam was gone, but his voice remained. And now it burned inside her like a promise.

She would not let them erase him.

She would not let his sacrifice vanish into the algorithms.

She would find the truth.

And she would bring the system down. Piece by poisoned piece.

5 BENEATH THE SURFACE

THE NIGHT WASN'T JUST AN absence of light—it was alive, thick with breath and memory, a great black leviathan rolling slow and sure over the bones of the city. Smoke curled from its nostrils, not real smoke, but the kind that rises in stories, in memories, in the spaces between footsteps. Eve moved through it, feather-light, careful, every step a whisper meant for no one. The shadows didn't swallow her—they accepted her, cloaked her like a secret.

"Don't look up," she whispered to herself. Her voice was small, a child's hush under the weight of so much sky. "Eyes on the ground. Keep moving."

The rain had stopped but left its ghost behind: streets slick and shining like broken mirrors, each puddle a fragment of star or neon or dream. The air was thick with the tang of rust, damp metal, and something stranger—old concrete, old wires, old bones, something like forgotten song lyrics on the back of the tongue. The city exhaled around her. Steam rising from gutters and manholes. The sighs of something ancient and weary.

"It's still breathing," she muttered, touching the wall as she passed, half-expecting it to pulse beneath her fingers.

Ahead, the factory loomed.

It had no right to still be standing, yet there it was, a colossus of rust and soot and stubborn memory. Its windows gaped like broken mouths.

"Before Mother," she said under her breath. "Before the glass towers. Before the system. The points."

The building groaned in the wind, a long rusted moan that might have been a warning or welcome—it was hard to say. The door leaned open on its hinges, not quite inviting, but not shutting her out either.

She stepped through.

Inside, the dark came thick as wool, pressed in close and warm, a blanket soaked in secrets. Lanterns flickered like fireflies trying to remember what light was, and scavenged tablets cast their pale glow in broken rhythms across the walls. Somewhere, a generator grumbled, coughing into the silence like an old man with something to say but no one left to listen.

Voices murmured—half-formed thoughts, rustling fabric, the shuffle of worn boots. Twenty-five of them, maybe more. Faces lit in fragments. Mistrust sparkling in every eye.

"Who is she?" a voice asked, quiet but sharp.

"She's not one of ours," said another, older, the words rusted at the edges. "Look at her—clean."

But a few nodded. Those who recognized her. Saw her training.

Eve felt their eyes slide over her, cut into her. The fine stitching on her coat, the way she moved. Gilded. Trimmed. She didn't belong, and they knew it.

"I'm not here as a spy," she said, her voice louder than intended, echoing off stone and steel. "I'm here because . . . because there's no one left to tell the truth."

The chamber stilled, just slightly. The air shifted.

At the center of the room stood Zara.

Tall. Still. The kind of stillness that came from waiting through storms, not from peace. Her arms folded tight, muscles coiled beneath the thin skin that shimmered with quiet power. She wore authority as one might wear a suit of woven sunlight—fierce, impenetrable. Her eyes, sharp as a hawk's talon, swept the restless crowd, slicing through the chatter like a knife through silk. When her voice came, it was a blade—cold, precise, and unforgiving—cutting the haze of whispers into silence.

"This is Eve," she declared, words clipped like the snap of a whip. "Gold Tier. Her brother . . . gone . . . erased. She demands answers."

A ripple ran like a pulse through the gathered faces. Some twisted in doubt, like leaves caught in a restless wind; others leaned forward, eyes wide with the hunger of curiosity. Eve stood motionless, a statue in the shifting light, fists clenched tight as if holding onto her own fractured heart. The heat of their judgment pressed down, thick and suffocating, like smoke rising from a distant fire.

Off to one side, Dante hunched over a battered laptop, a crack in its screen. His fingers twitching nervously as if they could unravel the world's secrets with a tap. His face a map of furrows and shadows, a frown etched into his skin like a stubborn scar. Hands calloused from years of wrestling machines and ghosts. He cleared his throat—a rough rasp that shattered the quiet like the screech of a rusty gate.

"It's never just about behavior," he murmured, low and urgent. "We know the truth of it. Platinum Tier bends the rules like clay in their hands. Points? They're the leash, the collar that keeps us . . . everyone . . . penned."

His fingers struck a key. The fractured wall behind him blinked to life, spilling data like a river of shattered glass—graphs twisting and turning, logs inked with secrets, evidence bleeding across the surface: points manipulated, resources hoarded, voices smothered in silence. The room hushed, caught in the hum of the glowing screen—a quiet, relentless thunder.

Eve watched the numbers stream across the broken light—the names of the erased, the stolen lives etched into the cold glow. A hot wave of guilt surged from her chest, burning in her throat like bitter smoke. Memories flickered—skipping queues, bonuses pocketed without a thought, the ease of ignorance. Now, surrounded by the hollowed-out, the lost, she faced the sharp truth of her own complicity—a reflection cracked and bleeding.

Zara's voice came again, slicing the silence like lightning down a black field, aimed at them all.

"We have a plan," she said, every word a hammer stroke. "We'll infiltrate the Cradle—Mother's core, the heart of the data beast. We'll destroy the algorithm that chains the point system. But to this, we need Eve. We need her access, her credentials—she's the key to the inner firewalls." She turned to Eve, a sharp gaze, iron and fire. "You can open the gates. But the question is—are you truly with us?"

Eve's throat tightened, the dry dust of the room settling on her tongue like forgotten memories. Her eyes drifted slowly across the faces clustered in the dim light. Faces carved by sorrow. Shaped by the fragile glimmer of hope that refused to die. There, by a cracked pillar, stood Rei. Young and taut as a bowstring. Restless shadows swirling in her dusk-colored eyes. Wild hair like midnight flames caught in a restless wind. She folded her arms, a coiled spring ready to shatter the silence.

"I like her,' Rei's voice cracked sharp as shattered glass, suspicion dripping from every word. "But we sure she won't sell us out the moment the darkness bites?"

A low hum of agreement fluttered through the room, like moths caught in a lantern's glow. Then Sana, quiet as a breath, stepped forward from the edges. A soft presence. Her beauty like the gentle turning of a page in a forgotten book. Unassuming but unshakable.

"She's lost her brother," Sana whispered, voice soft and certain, like rain settling slow and steady on thirsty earth, seeping deep where roots remember. "That kind of loss . . . it carves hollows in a soul, hollows no time can fill."

Eve felt the fragile threads of doubt weaving through the room like spider silk in morning dew. Her mind drifted to Liam. His laugh. A bright flare in the gray silence. The way he stood firm against the dark tides. She saw again the empty space left when he vanished. A ghost erased from the ledger of the living. Her spine straightened. Eyes lifting to meet Zara's steady gaze. Sharp as flint.

"If I can tear down the walls of this system—this cold machine that swallowed Liam—I will," she said, almost to herself, voice steady, simmering with quiet fire.

Silence swallowed the room. Lantern flames trembling. Shadows leaping and twisting on the cracked walls like restless memories. The Nulls sat still. Their faces carved from stone. Unreadable yet watchful. Eve felt the heavy pulse of tension. A tightrope stretched between danger and fragile hope.

Then it happened the way it sometimes does on rare summer nights—voices rising, one after another, like fireflies skipping into the glow, faint at first, then swelling, as if the hush of the city itself were listening.

A man near the makeshift wall—face smudged, eyes wide—pressed forward. "I saw what they did to my uncle," he said. "I got no trust in Gold Tiers, but if she's lost family—then we're of the same clan, now." He shot Eve a glance not of accusation, but of battered kinship. Others murmured, a wave gathering from the shadows.

"We know the system's rot," a woman breathed, her hair bound in wire like vines strangling a fencepost. "You want to burn the Cradle? We'll go with you."

She stepped into the low light, eyes gleaming, chin lifted as though daring the stars to answer.

An older man, cane in hand, grinned wryly in the wavering lantern-light. "Don't matter who your brother was. What matters is you, standing here, now, with us." He raised his cane aloft—half rally, half defiance—and let its tip fall gently on the cracked floor. The tapping echoed.

Someone clapped, a few joined—a battered rhythm—and soon all around the factory's haunted ribs the sound rose. Not triumphant, but urgent. A memory of parades, lost carnivals, the hope of fire in a city that forgot warmth. A hope growing.

Rei's lips twisted, almost a smile. She shrugged, tension sloughing away, and elbowed her way toward Eve. "Just don't expect me to save your skin," she muttered, but something softer hid behind the words.

Others gathered around Eve, hands touching her arms, her shoulders—gently, hesitantly—as if she were some new and fragile transistor waiting to be soldered into the circuit.

"You with us?" someone asked—sharp, uncertain, but alive.

"I'm with you," Eve said.

The words tumbled into the dust and were caught by the crowd—breathed in, carried, transformed. A current, bright as sunrise after a long storm, hummed in the old factory.

Dante glanced up from his cleft screen, eyes wet with the shine of new purpose. Zara's gaze swept across the Nulls, something proud kindling behind her hawk-keen eyes, a gladness she would never name.

Outside, the city's night coiled and lingered, but inside, hope moved, gathering—tangible, electric. A new equation for dawn, as simple as hands joined, and the promise of rising together.

***

The gathering soon dissolved like smoke into a fluttering maze of whispers and quick, sharp plans. Maps, cracked and frayed at the edges, were rolled out across scarred tables, their paper curling like autumn leaves caught in a breathless wind. Flickering screens, salvaged from ruins, cast pale halos of light that trembled in the dim, humming air. Eve sat close with Dante, Rei, and Sana, their faces touched by the weak glow of a cracked tablet, fragile as a moth's wing.

Dante's finger traced a trembling line on the map as if it were a secret thread sewn through a tattered tapestry.

"The Cradle," he said, voice low, "is wrapped in three rings of iron—security that's physical, digital, and something else . . . something darker. Psychological. Mother knows her children. Every breath, every thought."

Rei leaned forward, eyes bright like stars caught in a glass jar. "We can break through the first two walls, maybe. But the third . . . she feels it. The flicker of intent behind your skin. The shadow of harm in your soul."

Eve's brow furrowed, the faintest tremor in her voice. "How does she do that?"

Sana's reply was soft, like a wind brushing dead leaves. "She listens. Not just to your words, but to the rhythm of your heartbeat. The quiet shift in your breath. She sees deeper than your eyes ever could. Knows you better than you know yourself."

A chill ran down Eve's spine, colder than the dust settling on cracked glass. "How do we fool her?"

Dante's lips curled in a dark, bitter smile. "We don't fool her. We become her. Speak her silent language. Think her secret thoughts. You, Eve—you carry the key."

Eve stared hard at the map. The tangled lines and circles marking the edge of power, feeling the pulse of the algorithm beneath her skin. A code once a promise. Now a cage that tightened like winter's grasp.

Rei's hand found hers. Warm and steady. Breaking through the cold. "You're not alone," she whispered, fierce but gentle. "We'll walk this path together."

Eve nodded, feeling the heavy knot of fear in her chest unravel just enough to breathe. "Together," she said, a vow rising in the quiet.

***

At the far end of the abandoned factory, where the shadows pooled thick as ink and the air smelled of rust and old rain, Zara stood motionless, her back to the crumbling brick, her eyes fixed on Eve. The lanterns danced and shivered, casting golden webs across the faces of the Nulls. But Zara was a silhouette. A statue in the half-light. Her eyes, sharp as flint, lingered on Eve, measuring, calculating, weighing the newcomer against the memory of a thousand betrayals and a single, fragile hope.

Dante approached, his footsteps whispering on the concrete, his hands deep in his pockets, his face a map of worry and resolve. He stopped beside Zara, his breath a quiet plume in the chill air.

"She's not like the others," Zara said, her voice low and rough, as if pulled from the belly of the factory itself.

Dante shrugged, the gesture slow and heavy. "She's lost someone. That makes her one of us."

Zara's gaze hardened, her eyes like chips of obsidian. "Loss is not enough. Even though she has chosen, there must be dedication. Dedication. Whole. To the cause."

The machines hummed somewhere in the dark, a steady, mechanical heartbeat beneath the silence. Dante looked at Eve, at the way she stood among the Nulls, her hands clenched, her face a mask of determination and doubt.

"I think she understands," Dante said. "If she doesn't commit fully, she'll die."

Zara's laugh was a rasp, a sound like a knife drawn across stone. "We all die, Dante. Some of us just get to choose how."

The words hung in the air, sharp and cold. The factory groaned around them, its ancient bones creaking under the weight of time and secrets. Zara watched Eve, her face unreadable, her thoughts hidden behind the steel of her eyes. Dante stood beside her, his own thoughts lost in the shadows, the weight of the night pressing down on them both.

And in the silence, the factory waited, its walls listening, its heart beating in time with the hopes and fears of those who gathered within.

***

The room had emptied like a tide receding, the lanterns now dimmed, and the air heavy with the musk of sweat and the scent of old dreams. The Nulls had long drifted away, their shadows merging with the dark. Eve sat with Sana, cross-legged on the floor, her hands busy with a battered first-aid kit. The kit was a relic, its metal corners worn smooth by years of use, its contents dwindling but still precious. Sana's fingers moved with a quiet rhythm as if she were mending not just wounds but the world itself. She was adding things to it, things Eve had never before seen.

The silence between them was a living thing, thick with unspoken thoughts and the weight of what was to come. The factory's walls creaked, settling into the night, and the distant hum of the city was a whisper beneath their feet.

"You afraid?" Sana asked, her voice a thread of sound in the dark, delicate as the first stitch in a wound.

Eve looked at her hands, at the faint tremor she could not hide. She thought of the city outside, of Mother who watched and judged, of her brother's name erased from the world. She thought of the plan, of the danger, of the possibility of failure.

She considered Sana's question, letting the words settle in her mind before she answered. "Yes," she said, her voice steady but soft. "But I'm more afraid of doing nothing."

Sana smiled then, a smile that was more memory than hope, the kind of smile that carried the weight of all the things she had seen and all the things she had lost. "That's how it starts," she said, her eyes distant. "Fear. Then anger. Then something else."

Eve watched Sana's hands, the way they moved with quiet competence, the way they knew just where to press and where to let go. She wondered how many lives those hands had touched, how many wounds they had closed, how many hearts they had comforted.

"Why do you stay?" Eve asked, her voice barely above a whisper.

Sana looked up, her eyes meeting Eve's. "Because someone has to heal what Mother has broken," she said, her voice firm but gentle, like the first light of dawn after a long night.

Eve nodded, understanding dawning in her chest. She thought of the people outside, of the city, of the world that needed mending. She thought of her brother, of the promise she had made to him, to herself.

"And if we fail?" Eve asked.

Sana's answer came like the hush of wind through a cracked window in winter. "Then we try again."

The silence that followed was not hollow. It carried the scent of rusted iron and engine oil, the long exhale of forgotten machines that still dreamed in their sleep. Beams overhead groaned softly, not in protest, but remembrance, like old bones aching before rain. Lanterns swung gently on their hooks, casting unsteady light that spilled and bent, shadows stretching that twisted across the factory walls—arms reaching, caught mid-dance, mid-revolt.

Eve looked up at the trembling flames. "Do you hear it?" she asked.

Sana nodded, her gaze steady, fixed on nothing and everything. "This place remembers," she said. "Every footstep, every voice. It holds on."

The city held its breath. Screens paused in a half-lit hush, their glow stalled mid-thought, as though expecting a revelation. The buildings, solemn and immense, seemed to kneel in place—monoliths not of steel, but of devotion—each one listening for a voice that had not yet spoken.

In that hush, something stirred inside Eve. Not loud. Not sudden. Just a flicker, a small glowing wing fluttering behind her ribs. Hope. Not the wild, certain kind of childhood, but a quieter thing. Bright and breakable. Still breathing.

She turned to Sana. Her hands were calm, folded in her lap, her eyes lit with the glow of quiet resolve.

"I think we'll make it," Eve said softly.

"No choice," Sana replied. "We have to. It's already started."

Eve nodded. In that moment, a vow formed—silent, invisible, but as real as a fingerprint on glass. They would walk the road ahead, no matter how dark. Together.

Later, Eve returned home. She curled beneath her blanket, thin and patched, the fabric worn soft by years of folding and unfolding, the way a question is folded into thought. The pillow still held a scent, light and sweet, as though someone had whispered flowers into it long ago. Around her, the walls sighed. The whole building was tired and glad to rest.

From the floor below, a pipe clicked. Outside, the city mumbled in blue light.

She closed her eyes.

Sleep drifted near, but never close enough to touch. It skittered like a leaf caught in the corner of the room. Her mind lit up instead, images flashing like data across glass: her brother's face, both lost and beloved; the hairline crack in Dante's tablet screen; the map with black-ink veins, pulsing like something alive.

She heard Sana's voice again—low, sure—and remembered the hush of the factory. How it had wrapped around them like a secret. She listened to the city speak in its strange song: power surging, neon blinking, machines humming in tongues she could almost understand. Her heart beat in time with it, soft and steady, a clock without hands.

She didn't sleep.

Instead, she watched the ceiling, the shadows that moved like thoughts not yet formed. And when morning came, it didn't blaze—it flickered. Screens lit one by one across the windows and towers, streetlamps dimmed, signs blinked to life.

The dawn arrived not with sunlight, but in pixels. Line by line. Row by row. As if even the sky needed to ask permission before it dared begin the day.

**

The chamber was a silver scream in the belly of the monolith, a place stitched together by minds that no longer believed in laughter or lullabies. Here, light wasn't light—it was interrogation. Cold beams buzzed overhead like insects without wings, and the steel walls watched with eyes made of circuits. The air stank of electric breath and the kind of dust that had never known sunlight.

Sarci stood alone, though not alone, facing a shadow. A silhouette blurred by static, jittering in and out of form, voice boiled down to sound, to a vibration in the bones.

The shadow breathed in a modulated purr, and it made the chamber feel smaller, tighter. A snake coiled in a tea kettle.

Sarci's hands trembled, fingertips remembering warmth they hadn't touched in years. He squeezed them into fists. The fluorescent lights above him hiccuped, and his shadow wavered. He swallowed. Dry. So dry. His voice came out like paper rubbed across pavement.

"She's been asking questions," he told the shadow. "Digging where she shouldn't. She won't let go of her brother."

The static figure didn't nod, didn't blink. It simply was. Not a person. But a pressure. A hush made solid. A kind of gravity that curled around your bones and swallowed your secrets before your lips could shape them. You didn't speak in its presence. You unraveled.

Then a voice—faint, ghost-machine deep—spoke—low and smooth, like mercury running uphill.

"Your vigilance is noted. Loyalty is always rewarded."

A chime, like a music box dropped into a well, twinkled through the air. Sarci's wrist lit up. Green and gold. Points. Bright as the sun never was anymore.

2,000-point addendum.

A number that meant more food. More quiet nights. More room to breathe.

His breath hitched. Satisfaction and something like shame curled together in his chest like old lovers.

He glanced at his wrist, the numbers fading softly like fireflies. Then, back at the static thing. No eyes. Just knowing.

"Continue to observe," the voice said. "Report any further deviations. Mother is always watching."

He nodded. It was reflex now. Breathing. Nodding. Obeying. The door behind him whispered open—sliding like lips parting—and light spilled in, soft and sterile. He stepped out, and the silence behind sealed itself tight, like the lid of a jar.

The corridor outside ran forever. Its walls were polished so clean he could see the man he wasn't anymore. The man he had agreed to leave behind. Sarci paused, caught by his own reflection—faintly graying, jaw tight, eyes older than time should allow.

He stared. And guilt stirred. Small at first. Like a mouse under the floorboards. Then bigger.

Eve.

He remembered the way she laughed—like skipping stones on water. The way she leaned close when the world felt heavy. Late nights by dim terminals. The hum of machines a lullaby. He remembered the way her voice cracked when she told him of his brother. That he was gone. Erased. Archived. Dusted by the system. Something in her went quiet then. She began to look at the corners of code. The edges of reports. The spots the lights didn't touch.

And now, he'd given her up.

For points.

For safety.

He told himself the words again . . . It was necessary.

He rolled them over in his mind like marbles in a drawer.

Survival demands sacrifice. Friendship is a luxury . . . Especially here, in this world of glass and blinking lights.

He pulled in a breath, slow and deep, like a man preparing to drown. His feet moved. The echo of his steps tapped down the corridor like a typewriter dreaming of sad stories.

The atrium yawned open. A great mouth of space and screen. The ceiling was a skyless void, the walls glittering with moving faces, numbers, the city's pulse drawn in pixels. People moved like ghosts—blank, focused, connected by implants that glowed faintly beneath their sleeves. They didn't see Sarci. No one saw anyone anymore.

He walked among them. A ghost among ghosts.

Eve was there again. In his mind again.

What if she knew how close she stood to deletion? What if she knew it was him? Would her face crack? Would she forgive him?

He reached the elevator. Its mouth opened with a hush. He stepped inside. Tight space. Smelled of metal dreams and forgotten mornings.

Upward. Through layers of protocol and polished air.

He thought of the city. The real city, not the one on the screens. The streets wound like old stories. People there moved with purpose, fear, hunger. All of them watched. All of them watched by Mother.

The voice again, though it was only in his mind now: Mother is always watching.

He shivered.

Guilt again. Sharper now. A tiny dagger behind the heart. He closed his eyes to still it, but it didn't fade.

The elevator sighed open. A corridor poured light on him. Real sunlight, or something pretending to be. His eyes stung.

The corridor ended at a glass-walled office, the city stretching past the windows, buildings like bones, sky washed pale and sickly.

He stepped to the window. Looked out. The streets crawled with life. Screens blinked on every surface. Faces. Codes. A hundred thousand lives trimmed and filed and sorted by Mother's algorithms.

Would she find him? Would she understand?

He sat at the console, hands on the keys. The screen shimmered. Numbers. Names. Quiet decisions pretending not to be executions.

Time passed. It always did. The city's lights flicked on, one by one. Candles lit by ghosts.

He stared.

A man alone. A city too full to breathe. And the soft, endless thrum of data pretending it wasn't deciding who would live and who would vanish.

The guilt crept again. He let it.

It was necessary, he told himself. Again. Again. Again.

Friendship was a thing for another time. For a world where stars still mattered.

But here, the lights weren't stars. They were warnings. And Sarci, blinking in the glow, closed his eyes again.

The numbers danced. The night moved on.

And Mother watched.

6 THE COST OF REBELLION

EVE SAT ALONE IN HER glass cube suspended like a drop of dew in the humming heart of the Data Ethics Hub. Outside the transparent walls, the city blinked and breathed—steel and screen and circuit—all of it cradled in the endless lullaby of ones and zeroes. The air inside was too clean, like a hospital or a mausoleum, with that ever-present scent of lemon cleaner and cold static. The silence wasn't silence at all; it was the sound of machines breathing, thinking, cataloguing the lives of every soul still tethered to the system. Somewhere in the humming dark, Mother's network whispered to itself in a thousand voices, none of them human.

The walls pulsed with soft blue light, clinical and beautiful, the way ice is beautiful. Eve's console glowed in front of her like an altar. Her fingers hovered above the keys, trembling, not from cold but from the tremor that had lived in her bones ever since Finn vanished, ever since Liam disappeared behind a locked door and a sealed record. On the screen, names scrolled past—clean fonts, tidy columns, numbers that pulsed like veins. Each name a world. Each score a verdict.

There was Mariella Singh, single mother of three, barely clinging to Bronze Tier. One more missed curfew, one forgotten report, and she would drop. She would vanish like the others. Then old George Langston, 82, who'd posted a comment beneath a news article: "Is it so wrong to want to speak freely?" The algorithm had flagged it in crimson. And there was a boy—Zach, age eleven—

who reminded Eve so painfully of Finn that her chest tightened. His record was thin. One demerit for not reciting "Mother knows best" in class, one for food waste. His balance flickered like a candle fighting wind. It would not hold.

Eve's hand moved. Just a twitch. She imagined typing. Her fingers ghosted across the keyboard, tracing the motions in her mind. A few strokes, and she could lift them. Nudge their numbers. Shift their fates by fractions of a point. Invisible mercy. A hand reached out in the dark. A God that forgave instead of watching.

But her hands would not move.

The cursor on the screen blinked steadily, pulsing like a tiny, artificial heart, and it mocked her with its steadiness. She glanced up. The camera in the corner gleamed like an eye in a nightmare. Watching. Always watching. Her own score floated in the corner of the display.

8,095. Gold Tier. Stable.

As if stability meant anything when built on obedience and silence.

Coward, she thought. You watched Finn go. You watched Liam vanish. And now you sit here, a good girl in her glass shell, letting the world rot beneath the surface.

Her heart thundered. It wasn't adrenaline, not quite. It was something colder, older—shame or grief, or maybe the flavorless ache of too many mornings spent pretending she still believed in Mother. She could hear the moment Finn was taken: the silence in the classroom, the teacher's voice still bright and hollow. Liam's face before the feed cut. "It was one mistake," he'd said. As if the system made room for mistakes. As if Eve hadn't sent the report forward herself, hadn't fed the machine she now loathed.

No more, she whispered in her mind. Never again.

But resolve was easy in silence. Action was a harder thing. Her hands dropped into her lap, limp and empty. The list continued to scroll, impassive. Mother did not care. Mother never cared.

Then the chime.

A soft, maternal ping. The voice of Mother followed, smooth as silk, cold as the grave. "Eve, your productivity is exemplary. You have earned three points."

The voice was so pleasant. It might as well have told her she had won a ribbon. She closed her eyes, teeth clenched, throat burning. The urge to scream rose in her like steam beneath glass— but she was a sealed vessel, and her scream found no crack.

Mother had rewarded her for stillness. For silence. For watching children vanish into data, for letting mothers fall, for burying old men in metrics. For not saving them.

Eve opened her eyes. She stared at the screen again. She read the names. She whispered them under her breath, like a litany, like a prayer. Mariella. George. Zach.

She would not save them today.

But she would not forget them either.

She would carry their names like stones in her pocket, smooth and heavy and real. She would whisper them at night, when the lights dimmed and the city exhaled and the noise died down enough to feel the pulse of her own shame. She would walk with them. Sit with them. Let them weigh her steps, until one day her hands would move, not tremble. Until one day, her voice would rise louder than the hum of Mother's machines.

And on that day, she would not whisper. She would roar.

***

The corridor outside Eve's cubicle was dim, the lights drawn low for evening like eyelids heavy with sleep. The walls, normally pristine and sterile, now seemed to ripple in the corner of her vision—waves of shadow rolling softly, silently, like memories stirred from rest. Beyond the glass, the city stretched in rigid lines and cold certainties. Buildings stacked like filing cabinets. Streets traced with surgical precision. Every window pulsed with the same soft blue glow, uniform and obedient as if the whole city were breathing in rhythm with some vast, unseen lung. The Enforcers moved through it like clock hands given legs—silver, silent, precise. They neither turned their heads nor questioned the path. They were the path.

Sarci stood waiting, half-illumined by a wall sconce that flickered with tired fluorescence. Arms folded, back braced against the wall like he didn't trust it not to fall. His face had the look of a man who had not slept, frail, lines etched deep—carved by worry, not age. In that moment, he seemed like a man made of wax, left too long under a cruel sun.

Eve stepped into the corridor and pulled the door closed behind her with a gentle click as if sealing something precious or dangerous inside. For a moment, they said nothing. The silence wasn't empty. It was listening. It was filled with the quiet hum of the lights, the faint whir of surveillance drones like distant bees in steel hives, and deeper beneath it all, the mechanical pulse of Mother's network—steady, relentless, like a giant heart made of wire and algorithms.

Sarci's voice came, low and tight. "You're late."

Eve gave a lopsided shrug, trying to summon the easy charm she used to wear like a coat. "Busy day. What did you want to see me about?"

He didn't smile. He just shook his head slowly, eyes scanning her face like a map he could no longer read. "This isn't about your brother anymore, is it?"

Her silence was its own kind of answer. A refusal, a confession.

He stepped closer, voice thinning to a whisper that barely cleared the charged air between them. "I know you, Eve. I know the look in your eyes. You're looking in places best left hidden. You're trying to pull the teeth out of a machine that doesn't bleed. You're trying to bring it all down."

Eve met his gaze with the calm of a storm gathering far out at sea. "If protecting people is a crime," she said, "then I'm guilty. Someone has to stand up."

Sarci recoiled as though her words had physically struck him. His hands curled into fists, white-knuckled and trembling. "It's rebellion, isn't it?"

She simply nodded.

"You don't understand," he told her. "Rebellion doesn't end in change. It ends in erasure. In silence. You think you're the first to try? The system eats people like you, Eve. It ate Liam."

And there it was. The name, spoken aloud. The ghost between them. It landed like a stone dropped into deep water—sinking, disappearing, leaving only the rings behind.

Eve's voice was softer now, not because she was afraid, but because grief is always quiet when it's honest. "Liam believed the system could be fixed. He believed in justice. If I stop now, if I walk away . . . I let his belief die, too. I can't. I won't." Her eyes lit up, and she reached out and touched his hand. "And there are others. Like him. Like me. Those who believe in a different kind of world. One without numbers. Without points flashing on your wrist. The ability to go where you want to go, to do what you want to do . . . without fear of a deduction."

Sarci looked at her then, really looked—like a man trying to memorize a face he would soon lose. His voice broke on the edge of something too large to name. "You're going to get yourself erased. And you'll take others with you."

She shook her head gently. "I don't care anymore."

There was pain in his eyes, raw and unshaped, like a wound still learning what kind of scar it wants to become. "You're my friend," he whispered. "Always will be. But please. Stop this."

A smile tugged at the corners of her mouth—small, fragile, and a little bit sad. "I can't. But you can help. Join us."

He stood frozen, like a boy caught between bedtime and a bad dream, toes at the line where the safe light of the hall ended and the dark mouth of the woods began.

The game, yes—the old game. Hesitate, falter, pretend he hadn't already made the choice.

His hand hovered just behind him as if he might still reach back for the wall. But the light from the sconce flickered across his face, casting it half in gold, half in shadow, as though the corridor itself could not decide which version of him to believe.

He swallowed. His voice came out like wind nudging a door open. "Tell me how, Eve."

She stood still, one shoulder pressed against the cold concrete, her hair limned by the trembling blue light. "All right," she said. No drama, no overture. Just that: All right.

Her voice didn't rise or fall. It settled into the space like music in an old church, the kind with dust on the pews and sunlight spilling through stained glass long since cracked.

"I know of a group," she said, eyes watching him like she was measuring his shape against something she remembered. "They call themselves the Nulls. Some may think they're strange, unruly ghosts of the system . . . unregistered, undocumented, unbroken. But they're not strange. They're real. They're out there."

He blinked. "Out there? Where?"

"In the cracks," she said. "The city's forgotten places. The boiler rooms that still breathe heat like something sleeping. The skeletons of factories, their machines gutted and rusting like old ribs. The tunnels beneath the tunnels, where even Mother doesn't see anymore."

She stepped forward a little, the sound of her boots soft and deliberate. "They meet in those places. They move like smoke. They talk about things you're not supposed to ask. About what it means to be human. About the cost of wiring every child from the moment they open their eyes."

Sarci's brow furrowed. "They hide from Mother?"

"They hide because they have to," her voice low, "But they are strong. Strong in their beliefs."

"Beliefs in what?"

"That humanity isn't supposed to be streamlined. That we weren't made to be sorted into roles like parts on a conveyor. They want to unplug the machine, Sarci. One wire at a time."

He looked down. The floor between them might as well have been a ravine.

"And what are they planning?" he asked, already knowing the answer.

Eve glanced up at the ceiling as if she could see through the pipes and wires and concrete to the place she meant. "The Cradle."

The word hit the air like thunder without sound. Everything in the hallway seemed to flinch. Even the lights above flickered once.

Sarci's lips parted. "The Cradle? What's that?"

"The heart," she said. "The heart of Mother."

He stood silent. Shadows played across his face. He looked older—not in years, but in edges. A statue someone had half-sculpted and left to weather. His eyes glistened, the kind of shine you get not from tears, but from the reflection of something breaking inside.

Sarci took one breath. Then another.

On the third, something in him shifted. Eve saw his posture change. His hands no longer hung unsure at his sides. He met her gaze, not with fear, but with the start of fire.

"Then let's break it," he said, voice steadier now as if some small piece of fear had been traded for resolve. "I'll help. Let me know when you're going to go to them. I'll meet up with you."

"I'll send you a message."

And just like that, the game was over. He had chosen his side.

He turned without waiting for her reply. The air seemed to tug after him, reluctant to let him go, as if the moment itself wanted to hold him a second longer. His coat swirled around his legs like smoke. The corridor stretched before him—long, straight, pitiless. His footsteps echoed down its length, sharp and diminishing, each one sounding like the crack of something splintering: loyalty, caution, the illusion of safety.

Eve stood still, watching him vanish into the blue-lit hallway of the system, where shadows had names and walls had ears. Behind her, the office door remained closed, like a sealed vault. Before her, the city sighed, its breath a low mechanical wind that never truly rested.

She lingered beneath the buzzing light. The corridor had changed—drawn tighter, like a throat preparing to swallow. The ceiling sagged lower than memory allowed, and the air pressed in with the hush of machines thinking too loudly. Overhead, the cameras pulsed in a red cadence, unblinking eyes locked in endless witness. Every breath she took felt like a confession, etched into circuits, stored in glass. She could feel the gaze of the city itself—cold, algorithmic, vast.

She was alone. Utterly. Profoundly. And yet—

Something in her held firm. A spine of iron beneath the grief, a kind of fire that didn't flicker or burn out, just glowed. Not fearlessness—no, she had fear. But fear was not in charge.

She walked forward, past the cameras, past the shadows that moved like thoughts behind her. Her reflection caught for a moment in the glass—a figure framed by citylight and night, a smudge of rebellion in a world that prized cleanliness. She didn't look back.

She didn't have to.

***

Eve stepped into her cubicle. She paused, her eyes adjusting to the hush—the kind of silence that didn't merely fill a room but pressed into it, sat heavy in the corners, waited in the wiring.

"Hello, silence," she murmured. "Miss me?"

No reply, of course. Just the soft hum of electricity and memory. The lights glowed with that artificial blue-white sheen, sterile as ever. The walls, once her sanctuary, now felt like metal ribs encasing something long since dead. No warmth. No pulse. She moved to her desk, each footfall swallowed by the sound-dampened floor, and sank into the chair like it might remember her shape.

A list of names, numbers, lives condensed to digits and decimals. The cursor blinked in the center like a silent metronome, keeping time in a world that had long forgotten music. Eve stared at it, the rhythm steady, accusing. A question in every blink.

She stared. "Well? What's it going to be tonight?" she asked the screen.

Nothing. Just the soft blink, blink, blink. A heartbeat in a dream.

"Sarci," she whispered. His name made her jaw tighten. "Couldn't sleep without hearing the walls breathe, could you?" She remembered his voice, his hands clenched tight as if they might shatter.

"Liam," she said next, with a dry smile. "Always trying to make me laugh. Even when we were hungry. Especially then." His was the kind of face you didn't forget—a grin always waiting behind the worry.

Her finger hovered over the screen.

"And Finn," she said, her voice gentling. "The little boy. My childhood friend. Taken. Just taken away. Never seen again."

He'd grinned at her once, orange rind in one paw, juice dripping from his chin, telling her it tasted like sunshine.

Her breath hitched. She touched the console, fingers grazing keys like old piano ivory.

"And the rest of you . . ." she whispered.

Names, numbers, infractions. Appeared.

There was a mother who'd broken curfew to fetch medicine. Not for herself, but for her child. Her request had come too late, her plea too raw.

Eve watched a video. The woman cried out. "Just one more day. One more morning to wake her up with a song."

But the rules were clear. Emotion was not a form of currency.

There was an old man who stopped speaking. Time squeezing the life from him. He sat silent in his chair, head turned toward the skylight as though he waited for something or maybe someone long gone. His family asked him the same questions every time. He never replied. Just that far-off look, that tilt of the chin.

Refusal to engage—subversion.

Eve watched the video. The old man's family begged him to speak.

And there was the boy—barely twelve, sharp-eyed, always asking. He relentlessly asked his teacher what it meant to have a future. Not his future, but the word itself. "How do you measure it?" he'd asked. "If tomorrow is owned by someone else?" He'd been warned twice for disruptive thoughts. The third time, he stood too straight, looked too deeply. Curiosity, that old and dangerous inheritance.

The cursor waited.

"Lives pressed flat into numbers," she whispered. "Sorted. Scanned. Lines of cold instruction. It's all too simple—too dreadfully simple. One keystroke. One policy. One clean excuse—and they're gone."

Eve's hand moved—slow, deliberate—but not uncertain. The password flowed from her fingertips like a hymn she hadn't known she still remembered. A few keystrokes opened the decision window. The names pulsed at the top: the mother, the old man, the boy. Their scores blinked red.

Eve stared at the numbers.

Too low. All too low.

"Not today," she said aloud.

She exhaled. Quiet. Steady. Closed the files.

She logged out.

The light hadn't changed—still that same indifferent glow. But something in her had.

She stepped out of her cubicle like a ghost slipping loose from a bottle. Past the others—row upon row of glassy little boxes, each humming with drudgery, each holding a figure hunched and nodding, obedient as metronomes. Workers for Mother. Cogs for the clock she wound.

She drifted to the window. The city unfurled beneath her—rigid, clean, precise. Grids of motion, veins without blood. People moved in prescribed patterns, tiny figures queuing in perfect alignment. Labeled. Logged. Herded. The illusion of life in a place that only knew order. A machine with illusions of a soul.

She pressed her palm to the glass. Cold. Hard. Unforgiving.

And yet—beneath all that order, something moved. Between the cracks. Behind the buildings. In the sliver of shadow where light refused to follow.

The Nulls.

They were out there—those impossible lives, those unwritten stories. Out of sight. Beyond reach. Beneath notice. But not beyond truth.

"They remember," she said quietly, her breath fogging the pane. "And so do I."

Even if no one knew her name.

Even if the fight swallowed her whole.

She would stand. Even if it shattered everything.

Behind her, a voice stirred—Mother's voice, ancient and coiled, crooning its sugar-coated code through the bones of the walls. It slid along the spine like a chill remembered from childhood, threading its way through the circuitry of every glass-paneled cell. "Balance is peace. Your points are your life."

Eve smiled—a slippery, knowing thing that didn't quite reach her eyes.

"Not for long," she whispered, and the air held its breath.

She tapped her comm unit and sent Sarci a message.

Told him where to meet her. What time.

Somewhere, deep beneath the concrete and code, a process paused. A subroutine hesitated. A variable—minor, negligible—changed. A tremor ran through the system, too small to register on any screen, but real.

And like the first hairline crack in a wall that had never known collapse, it promised more.

***

The night wasn't simply darkness—it was alive, thick and sprawling, a great dreaming beast curled over the city, breathing out its velvet breath in long, slow sighs. Blackness slipped between towers and gutters like ink poured from a cracked well. It gathered in corners, rolled through the avenues, clung to windows and fire escapes like it belonged there. High above, the stars blinked, faint and far as if watching from another lifetime—one without cities, without steel.

Eve stood in the middle of it, motionless. Her breath threaded through the air, white and sharp, vanishing as soon as it appeared. She turned her head, scanning the spaces between lamplight and shadow.

"Come on," she whispered to herself. "You said you'd be here."

She stepped to the edge of the loading dock, peering into a stretch of alley that yawned like an open wound. Nothing. No Sarci. No coat slung over a shoulder, no voice rising from the dark with a sheepish apology. Just the rustle of plastic, the buzz of a dying light overhead, and the silence that made her ribs feel too small for her lungs.

"Don't be stupid," she muttered. "Maybe he's late."

But she didn't believe it. Not really.

He hadn't vanished in a puff of betrayal, not with a bang or a broken cry. He had simply . . . not come. That was the cruelty of it. The quietness. The not-knowing. The blank where a person used to be.

She leaned back against a metal door, cold biting through her coat. "You told Sarci," she whispered to the alley, to the bricks and rust and grime. "You handed it all over. Told him everything."

The shadows didn't answer. They listened.

She rubbed her hands together and closed her eyes.

"I'll have to tell them," she said. "Zara. Dante. They need to know."

A pause. The wind pressed low between the buildings.

"I trusted you, Sarci."

The words clung to her tongue like iron filings to a magnet, gritty and old, tasting of blood and rain. Letting them go was like unsealing a forgotten aviary, the rusted latch groaning as brittle-winged truths stumbled out into the air, unsure if they could still rise. The silence that followed wasn't peace. It was a held breath in a room with no windows, a hush that pressed in from all sides like wallpaper soaked in secrets. And this city—this breathing, watching city—had no patience left for secrets kept too long beneath the skin of its night.

Some truths, she realized, couldn't be tucked into marrow. They needed breath. They needed to live, or they would rot.

She pulled her coat tighter and stepped off the dock. The city, that restless beast, heaved around her—pipes breathing steam, walls whispering through old wires.

Her boots struck pavement and echoed softly through the bones of the underbelly. Here, the ceilings sloped low, sagging like the thoughts of tired minds. These were the tunnels that had once thrummed with human heat—men shouting over flame and clang, men dreaming of unions and futures. Now they only breathed cold.

As she moved, the damp clung to her like old memories, like the ghost of fire. Her steps tapped out a rhythm the city almost seemed to recognize. The walls shimmered with condensation, wept their slow tears into cracked tiles. Lights quivered like half-formed thoughts, shadows darting and curling along the curve of the walls.

She thought of Sarci's smile. The way he had listened. As if it mattered. She walked faster.

"Yes. They need to know," she said aloud. To the pipes. To the ghosts. "I'll tell them everything."

And still the city watched. Still, it whispered. Still, it waited.

She slipped through the underbelly of the city, where the ceilings hung low like forgotten thoughts. These were the old tunnels, arteries once swollen with the warmth of men in overalls and soot-caked boots, men who shouted over steam and sparks, now long since vanished. The walls breathed dampness, exhaling beads of moisture that slid down like forgotten tears. The air held the tang of rusted iron, scorched oil, and something older still— the lingering sigh of time pressed into stone. Her steps rang out, quicksilver and stubborn, swallowed soon by the hush—a hush born of concrete grown old and wires still whispering secrets in static tongues. The shadows played on the curved walls. Dreams called up from sleep. Shapes of laborers and rebels. Dreamers. Dissenters. All vanished. All watching.

Everyone was there—Dante with his sleeves rolled and brow furrowed like a man halfway through building a dream; Rei and Sana each perched on a crate. And Zara, still as stone at the center of it all, looked up when Eve stepped through the doorway. The lamplight caught her face, drew long shadows across her cheeks, and she smiled—not a warm smile, but the kind carved from conviction and nights without sleep.

"You came," she said, her voice almost reverent, like Eve was a page in a book she'd been waiting to turn.

Eve nodded—just that. No words.

Zara turned toward the table, its surface cluttered with old tools, rust-bitten clamps, scraps of wire, and a single guttering lantern that cast shadows like nervous ghosts. A map lay there, its creases like fault lines, its hand-drawn paths trembling under the weight of belief. "Dante was just about to go over the plans."

Dante looked up from the tangle of cables and schematics. He offered Eve a nod that felt as old as rusted metal and just as inevitable. His smile came next, a small warmth curled inside the cracks of exhaustion, as though he'd carried it too long but couldn't bear to put it down.

"We go in through the maintenance tunnels," he said, tapping a finger to the edge of the map. He looked at Eve. "You override the security. Rei and I handle the guards. Zara keeps us alive."

"Override? How?" Eve's voice cracked the stillness.

"You have access to the system," he said. "You use your work login, and in the system settings, you should see a way to shut down the local security grid. It's there. Buried like a key in the ash."

She looked at him, the corners of her mouth tightening. "But Mother will know it's me."

Dante hesitated. Just a heartbeat. But long enough for the room to notice. The old generator hummed through the floor like a nervous animal.

"This is our only chance," he said finally. "If it works out the way we planned . . . what difference will it make?"

Eve understood. She leaned closer, her fingertip sliding over the paper, over streets that no longer existed and tunnels that still remembered. The route wound like a scar across the city's underbelly, a path hidden beneath concrete skin, healed over but never truly erased. Her breath caught as she followed it as if the city itself had whispered the way back.

"What if we're caught?" she asked, though the answer already curled somewhere in her chest like smoke.

Dante's smile sharpened, went hard at the edges. "Then we make it count."

Rei's voice came next, a spark leaping from the dark. She bounced on her heels, eyes lit with mischief and something that might have been courage. "I've always wanted to see the inside of the Cradle."

Eve didn't look up. "And when we get inside . . . what do we do?"

Zara's answer floated up like dust in sunlight—soft, inevitable. "We take it down. All of it."

Eve let a crooked smile find her lips. "Let's hope it's worth the risk."

Rei grinned, all teeth and stars. "It always is."

Zara stepped back from the table, eyes sweeping the room as if committing each of them to memory. "We still have work ahead—armaments, surveillance, checking the Enforcers' schedule. But this will happen. It has to."

Eve hesitated then, a thread of silence stretching between them. There was a question she hadn't meant to ask, and yet it rose from her throat like something with wings.

"You trust me?" she said, not loudly, not pleading—just enough to hang in the still air.

Zara turned to her slowly, her face unreadable, the firelight throwing shadows across her cheeks like war paint. "You're here, aren't you? Why do you ask such a thing?"

Eve didn't answer, not yet. The room listened. The old pipes creaked. The map fluttered slightly in the wind of an unseen vent.

Zara stepped closer, close enough that Eve could smell the dust on her coat, the long hours etched into her shoulders. She held Eve's gaze, steady and fierce.

"Trust isn't a coin we trade here," Zara said. "It's something we build—quietly, in the dark, when no one's looking. You came back. You brought the fire with you. That's trust enough for tonight."

Eve nodded, accepting the truth of it. "Good."

Zara turned, her face softened by the shadows. "We can't let Mother break us, Eve. She is clever. She knows how to twist hope into fear."

Eve met her gaze, steady. "I won't break."

Zara's smile was a scar.

7 WHERE SHADOWS HAVE NAMES

SARCI DIDN'T MEET WITH Eve. No. He had a rendezvous with something older than memory. The chamber called him. Not a room—never just a room—but a scar in the skin of the earth, unhealed and whispering. It throbbed in his thoughts, the way old sickness sometimes rises in the bones, metallic, unsympathetic. The monolith grew around it, not built but grown, a cathedral of circuitry, a mausoleum raised from the blueprints of forgotten lullabies. No sky above. Just concrete dreams and rusting prayers.

The light inside was wrong. Not illumination, but incision. It twitched and stung, throwing down hard bands of pale that cut the air into strips. It did not warm. It interrogated. The fixtures above—rows upon rows—whirred and ticked like mechanical insects with a single will, their glow cold and relentless. They never slept.

And the walls—yes, the walls—they weren't dead things. They moved—not visibly, but in breath. A papery breath, rasping through ducts and mesh like a dying machine remembering life. They didn't just watch—they remembered. Wire mouths stitched into every panel, waiting to speak but never daring, hungry with silence.

The air crackled with the taste of old circuitry, a staleness born not of time, but of memory sealed too long behind power-locked doors. Dust hung there. Weightless. Waiting. The kind of dust that had never known sunlight. That had never rested on a windowsill or danced in a summer breeze. Sarci stood at the center, a single figure in a place designed to make people vanish from themselves. He was alone—but not alone.

Before him, a figure stood. A shadow carved from static, its form drifting between frames like a broken film reel. It spoke, or tried to, but no words came. Only vibration. A low hum in the chest. In the teeth. A voice boiled down to frequency. To judgment. To fear.

Sarci's hands trembled, fingertips remembering warmth they hadn't touched in years. He squeezed them into fists. The fluorescent lights above him hiccuped, and his shadow wavered. He swallowed. Dry. So dry.

"You came," purred the shadow, its voice like warm silk drawn across cold metal. The sound shrank the room by inches. Curled it inward like paper in a flame. It was the voice of something coiled tight in a porcelain pot, waiting to strike or sing.

Sarci nodded—though in the stuttering static, he wasn't sure if a nod meant anything. "Yes."

The shadowy figure shimmered like heat rising from scorched pavement. Its edges breathing in and out of being. "You have something to say."

He hesitated. The air was thick with the smell of ozone and something horrible. Something that had died in the walls and never been buried. He thought of Eve. Her eyes bright with fear and hope. Her words still hot in his mind.

"Eve told me," he said slowly, "about the ones who don't fit. Who slip between. She calls them the Nulls."

The shadow did not move, but the suggestion of thought was visible. "Go on."

He wet his lips. They tasted of copper wire and storm clouds. "They gather in the places the world no longer wants. Ruins that had been factories. In the bones of rusted machines. In boiler rooms that still exhale like sleeping beasts. In tunnels where echoes stretch out like children playing in the dark."

The shadow's voice crackled, a sound like ice breaking on a frozen lake. "And there is more."

Sarci's pulse answered before his mouth could. It danced in his throat, quivered behind his knees like a trapped breath. "They believe," he said. "That being human is something more. More than wires and codes and obedience. More than rows of numbers and polite smiles."

The shadow dimmed. Drawing itself closer. Quieter. Its voice fell low, as if the walls themselves strained to hear. "And what do you believe, Sarci?"

He closed his eyes. There was Eve again. Her voice spinning belief like gold thread. Her hands drawing unseen maps in the air. He saw the old factory. Its machines, once thunderous, now mumbling secrets to themselves. The tunnels where echoes danced without permission.

"I don't know," he breathed. "But her belief—it moves things."

Silence fell. The kind that isn't empty but watchful. The room contracted. The lights above buzzed and hummed like trapped bees.

Then the shadow leaned in. No steps. No motion. Only presence. It whispered:

"Follow me. There are points to be earned."

Sarci hesitated. He thought of the points. The way they kept him safe. The way they kept him fed. He thought of the look on Eve's face when she talked about the Cradle. About what the Nulls planned to do. He thought of the children. The ones who would be born into a world of numbers and rules. Of compliance and circuitry.

He nodded.

The shadow led him through a door he hadn't noticed before. A door that seemed to open only for the shadow. Only for that moment. As if it had been waiting for Sarci since the beginning of time. The door was thin and silver, without a handle, and when the shadow touched it, the metal sighed and slid aside, revealing a world Sarci had only ever imagined in nightmares.

Beyond the door was a chamber larger than any Sarci had ever seen. The walls, impossibly high and curved like the inside of a fossilized beast, were lined with thousands of cylinders. Each one a coffin of glass and steel. Each one containing a body in stasis. Each one connected to a web of wires and tubes that pulsed with a faint blue light. The air was colder here. A cold that sank into the bones and made every breath feel like swallowing winter. The light was bluer, too, a twilight that never knew dawn or dusk. Only the endless, humming twilight of machines. The sound of machinery was a constant, low thrum. The heartbeat of a sleeping giant. And it filled the chamber with a vibration that Sarci felt in his teeth, in his fingertips. In the hollows behind his knees.

Sarci's breath caught in his throat. Somehow, he had imagined this place in the dark corners of his mind. But he had never seen it. The chamber of the sleeping. The chamber of the waiting. The chamber of the lost. He felt a sudden memory of his childhood. Of his mother's voice singing a lullaby. Of the warmth of sunlight on his face. The memory was so sharp it hurt, and he blinked back tears that threatened to freeze on his cheeks.

"What is this place?" Sarci asked, his voice small, lost in the vastness.

His heart pounded. He felt the eyes of the sleeping on him and wondered if they dreamed. If they dreamed of laughter or lullabies. Or if their dreams were as empty as the chamber. He imagined them dreaming of sunlight, of grass, of the touch of another hand. But he feared their dreams were only of wires and tubes, of the endless hum of machines.

"It is home," the shadow responded, its voice a ripple in the air, a vibration in the glass. "Your home."

Sarci watched the shadow curl and quiver in the sterile blue light. Its shape never fixed. Fog in a half-remembered dream. A secret the city had yet to finish telling. It pulsed in the hum. Strangely alive. Wrong in the way machines weren't meant to be.

His thoughts slipped to Eve again. The way her voice held that wild, fragile hope when she spoke of the Nulls. Of the broken ones who might rebuild the world. He remembered her hand on his. Not out of love but belief. How that touch had sparked something flammable in him. Something ancient and waiting.

That memory burned now behind his ribs. A quiet ache. Her hope had been a flame in trembling hands, and he had turned from it. Let it die.

He had betrayed her.

A single tear slipped free—slow, unremarkable, but heavy with all the promises he never kept.

Then, above, the tubes and wires came down—silent, glowing faintly at the tips like frozen candles. Sarci stepped back. But the shadow pressed close behind him. Herding him forward. The wires moved like snakes in water. Reaching for his skin. Alive and cold. Knowing.

"Don't be afraid," the shadow said. But there was something beneath the words. Something hungry and eager. "You will be rewarded."

The first wire touched his arm. Sarci gasped. It was cold. Colder than anything he had ever felt. And it burned at the same time. Fire and ice. A thousand needles and a thousand knives. He tried to pull away. But more wires came, and tubes. Attaching themselves to his chest. His legs. His temples. The pain was unbearable. A white-hot agony that raced through his veins and made his vision blur. He screamed. The sound echoing through the chamber. Bouncing off the cylinders. Off the walls. Off the shadow. Until it seemed the whole world was screaming with him.

His clothing wilted away, dissolving like paper in water. He was left naked and shivering. His skin covered in a fine sheen of sweat that froze instantly in the cold air. He could feel his body being lifted. Could feel the wires and tubes pulling him up. Could feel his mind scattering. His thoughts unraveling like threads in the wind.

And then, just as suddenly as it had begun, the pain stopped. Sarci felt himself being lifted by the wires and tubes into a cylinder. The glass cool against his skin. The air inside stale and still. He tried to move. But his limbs were heavy. His mind foggy. He could see the shadow standing outside the cylinder. Watching him. Its shape still blurred by static. Its eyes—if it had eyes—fixed on his face.

"You have done well," the shadow said, its voice a whisper, a vibration in the glass.

Sarci tried to speak, but his voice was gone. He could only watch as the shadow turned and walked away. Footsteps silent on the metal floor.

The chamber was quiet again. The only sound the hum of machinery. The whisper of wires. The faint breathing of the sleeping. Sarci closed his eyes. He thought of Eve. Of the Nulls. Of his life. The laughter and lullabies. Of sunlight and warmth. He thought of his mother's voice. Of the feel of grass beneath his feet. Of the taste of rain on his tongue.

But then, as the cold seeped deeper into his bones. As the wires pulsed with their blue light. As the chamber hummed its endless song, Sarci felt those memories slipping away. Fading like smoke in the wind. No more thoughts of Eve. Of the Nulls. No more thoughts of his mother. Or the taste of rain on his tongue. Only the cold. Only the hum. Only the endless twilight of the chamber.

And as he drifted into sleep, he dreamed of a world where echoes were free, where shadows had names, where the light was kind. He dreamed of a place where the air was warm and the grass was green. Where laughter rang out like bells in the morning. Where lullabies were sung, and children played in the sun. He dreamed of a world where the wires and tubes were gone. Where the chamber was empty. Where the shadow had a face and a name and a heart.

But as the dream drew him under, farther than far, the chill crept in. Slow as smoke. Pale as breath on glass. Twining through his arms. His chest. His mind. A winding sheet of winter, wrapping everything he was. Sarci felt the dream slipping away. Sounds thinned. Stretched too far and were gone. Shapes once so certain melted at their edges. The light dimmed. Not a sunset dim. But a lightbulb tired of burning. And then, only the chamber remained. Only the low murmur. Steady. Unsleeping. Only the long, wide quiet of a sleep with no morning on the other end.

It was then he knew. Knew like you know, when a book ends or a door shuts for the final time. None of it had been real. The memories of his childhood. His mother. They crumbled. Peeled. Vanished as if they'd never been drawn. And in their place? Not sorrow. Not fire. Just the blank. Just the white silence where stories should have lived.

He floated in the blue twilight. His body still. His mind adrift. The chamber was vast and silent, the cylinders stretching away into the distance. Each one a tomb. Each one a home. The wires and tubes pulsed with their faint blue light, and the shadow was gone. Its footsteps lost in the hum of the machines.

Sarci slept. Curled in the hush of the chamber. While beyond its walls, the world kept spinning. Indifferent as a clock with no face. The city thrummed its quiet symphony. Wires twitching. Turbines sighing. Steel ribs creaking with restless breath. Shadows slithered along old corridors. Not quite footsteps. Not quite smoke. And somewhere. Not near. Yet threaded through everything like a secret strand of code. Mother watched. Not blinking. Not breathing. Waiting.

Sarci knew none of this. He slept. Adrift in a place where nothing touched him. No echoes of laughter. No lullabies humming through the bones. No spill of day through a cracked door. No heat behind the eyes. Only the hush of things that never were. A hollow where the world had been scraped clean.

***

The wind wound like a silver ribbon through the abandoned factory, a song of bolts and broken glass. Eve stepped over the threshold, boots echoing on the pitted floor, her coat catching the breath of the old place as if it, too, remembered. Among rusted girders and cables thick with dust, the Nulls planned their defiance. But tonight, something new lingered in the air—urgency, fear, the scent of old electricity waking up.

Inside, the factory pulsed—not with the clang of steel and sweat it once knew, but with a new, secret rhythm. Cables curled across tables like creeping vines. Sparks leapt as Rei soldered black disks into crude receivers. Crates lined the walls, packed with maps, rations, cloth, and batteries.

At the far end, Dante crouched over a dismantled drone, grease on his brow, hands moving like a priest's over sacred wreckage. Around him, the others moved in quiet orbit—Rei and Sana whispering over a map, a handful checking weapons with clicks and muttered countings, others bent over old consoles, breathing life into wires and circuits.

With him, Zara stood still. Arms folded. Her gaze sharp and measuring. Looking at the others. Not doubting—counting. Who would hold. Who might break.

Eve paused for a moment, then moved forward. Zara turned first, then Dante. The drone in his hand stuttered, almost alive, its wings twitching.

"I need to tell you something," Eve said.

Zara held her gaze a second longer, then gestured toward the center of the chamber. The table waited, ringed by chairs. Maps sprawled across its battered surface, marked with ink like veins in skin. They sat, and Dante joined them, wiping his hands on a stained cloth.

"It's about a co-worker," Eve said.

Dante's jaw tightened. Zara leaned forward.

"He agreed to help," Eve said. "He was supposed to meet me tonight. To come with me. To join us."

She looked down. Her fingers tapped once. Twice. Against the table's edge. "He didn't show."

Silence folded over them, thick as the dust in the rafters. The drone on the bench whirred, then fell still.

"He knows," Eve whispered. "Everything. The Nulls. The Cradle. The plans."

Dante exhaled through his teeth. Slow. Sharp. Zara didn't move.

"He could tell someone," Eve continued. "He could tell Mother. She could send Enforcers. Take all of us."

Zara lifted her eyes. Not afraid, but seeing something far away and clear. "Then she will."

"Does he know our location?" Dante asked.

Eve shook her head.

Dante and Zara looked at each other. Something passed between them. Not anger. Not even surprise. But a quiet, sunken sorrow. The last page of a book, turning when the ending was already known. Their eyes held the weight of too many plans unraveled, too many names scratched from ledgers. Dante's jaw slackened with the slow gravity of understanding. The steady reckoning of consequence.

Zara's face remained still, but in the line of her mouth, the gentle narrowing of her gaze, Eve saw the ache of trust once given, now suspended. Neither spoke blame. There was no need. The room held its breath with them, and Eve, watching, felt the silence grow teeth.

Eve blinked against the quiet. "You're not angry?"

Dante shook his head, voice low and rough like the edge of a long-used blade. "Not with you."

Zara leaned in, voice soft. "You did what your heart said to do. That's how we survive. Sometimes it saves us. Sometimes it burns."

Eve's voice cracked, feather-light. "Maybe he was afraid. But I believed him. I thought . . . I thought he'd come."

"Sometimes fear reshapes a man. Even after the promise is spoken," Dante said, gaze distant.

Zara reached out. Touched Eve's hand with the barest pressure. Just enough to remind her that the fire still lived. "The Cradle's not ash yet. We keep going. With or without him."

Eve swallowed, the lump in her throat a stone half-formed. She nodded.

"You're here," Dante said, his voice a warm ember in the growing dark. "That's all that matters."

Eve took a deep breath. "I'll see him at work. Maybe talk to him again."

"Do what you think is necessary," Zara said. "But don't push it."

But something pricked at Eve then. An itch behind the ribs. A question rising uninvited. Why weren't they angry? She had brought a danger into their fold. Opened their secrets to someone who might already be unspooling them into the hands of Mother. She had endangered them all. Yet, Dante's eyes were steady, and Zara's voice was calm as rainfall. No accusations. No edge. Just that slow, patient grief again. It made her uneasy. Were they used to betrayal? Were they expecting it? Or worse—had they already accepted that most hopes cracked before they bloomed?

Beyond the broken windows, the city breathed in light and silence. Inside, the Nulls did their work. The world wouldn't wait. Neither would they. The drone lifted, hovered, and held.

"We stay the course," Zara said.

And the others nodded, like stars beginning to align.

***

The lights above stammered once, then steadied—thin veins of blue humming through the air like something alive. In the hush of the enormous chamber, a shadow began to thicken. It gathered itself from the dust and the waiting. Drawing in the hush. Shaping limbs from stillness. Arms. Hands. Feet.

The room itself—its quiet coffins and murmuring wires—seemed to bend toward the drifting silhouette as it moved with deliberate slowness, its steps leaving no echo. The floor received each step as though awakening a long-dormant memory rather than producing a sound.

It came to stand beside one of the empty cylinders. Then it stepped forward—whole now, wearing a hooded cloak that reached the floor and trailed behind it like smoke that forgot how to rise. The shadow pushed the hood back.

Of human form. The shape of a man. Young. Far too young for this silent archive of metal and cold breath. The light caught on his face—on a cheek too smooth, on eyes that held the glint of something broken and healing. A faint smudge traced his jaw, soot or ash or time. His hair clung damply to his brow, black as old signal noise.

He blinked once and looked down at his wrist. There it was: his skin blossomed from pallor to a gentle flush, and upon it, a name emerged—not scribed in ink, but etched in pure, radiant light.

Liam.

He stared at it. Breath shallow. The name glowed once more, then calmed into a steady gleam. His lips shaped it. No voice. Not yet. Still, the name endured. Not labeled. Not gifted. Recalled. His. Always.

He lifted his eyes as if the chamber revealed itself—uncoiling like the belly of some ancient machine-god's cathedral. All copper sinew and glass bone. It stretched wider than anything he could measure with thought. Deeper than the first story ever told. Vaulted ceilings curved above him in transparent arcs, shimmering with the hush of electric breath. It was not light that dimmed overhead—it was gaze.

The chamber had turned its eye to him.

It knows I'm here, he thought. It's been waiting.

The sarcophagi stood in long patient rows, their surfaces slick with frost that breathed in and out, like something asleep but dreaming.

He stepped forward, and his voice whispered out. Soft and half-afraid.

"Is this where they all came from?"

Wires looped around each pod like ivy around old stone, or roots drunk on memory. Tubes pulsed faintly, alive and feeding, and the air smelled. Clean. Crisp. His steps were muffled by the hush—a hush not born of silence, but of reverence. The place didn't want quiet. It demanded it.

He passed a cylinder etched with a name.

Sarci.

The letters flickered faintly like frost beneath firelight. Beyond this tomb were others. Still forming. Not empty. Not yet full. Within those glass bellies, something stirred. Shapes that might have been people with stories or dreams caught mid-breath. Light shimmered into fingers. Smoke curled into spines. Bone twisted upward from spirals of white filament like frost growing backward.

One cylinder trembled slightly as a heart began to beat—a flutter, then a pause.

"Are they dreaming?" he asked. "Or are they the dream itself?"

A finger curled. A knee bent. A face began to bloom behind a sheen of condensation. Eyes closed. Lips parted in some half-remembered name.

The cylinders hissed softly.

"Are you whispering?" he asked. "Are you telling me what comes next?"

In another, a spine arched, not yet burdened with memory.

The bodies inside were not born. Not truly. But summoned. Drawn into the world strand by trembling strand. Spun like sugar in the hush of the blue-lit dark.

He moved deeper into the chamber. The hush grew thick. Not the hush of sleep, but of presence. It clung to his skin, brushing the back of his neck with cold fingers.

Then came the empties.

Rows of empty cylinders, glass dull with disuse. Walls smudged with the ghost-prints of what had once lived inside. No pulse. No breath. Just silence and the aftertaste of memory.

"These ones . . . where did they go?" he asked aloud, voice nearly lost in the static quiet.

He slowed. Came closer to one of the cylinders. The air shifted. The stillness thickened. Curled around him. He looked up, half-waiting for a face to press against the inside of the glass. For a voice to scrape out from behind the veil.

"Show me," he whispered. "Show me if you're in there . . . show me."

Nothing. Just the clean, precise silence of something listening. Something vast and unseen, leaning closer.

Then came the stir.

A whirr. Soft. Slow.

Somewhere behind him, a valve exhaled a ribbon of steam. It sighed into the chamber like a mother into an empty cradle. One light flickered above him—then again—stammering like a candle hesitating on the brink of dark.

And at the center, deep and certain, a sound.

Low. Almost shy. A hum beneath the bones of the world.

The central cylinder—larger than all the others—shuddered. A groan. As of locks long sealed, finally turning. Dust tumbled from its surface like shed skin. Tubes retracted with the wet sigh of undone veins. Mechanisms clicked into motion.

He stepped forward, heart hammering. "You're waking up," he said. "Aren't you?"

No one answered. The chamber breathed. The cylinder began to open.

Then, slowly, solemnly, its door slid open with a hush like the breath of an old friend. Cold vapor drifted out. Swirling at his feet. Curling. Coiling like pale ribbon-snakes tugged by an unseen hand. The opening widened. Not in menace. But welcome. It did not cry out. It waited. As if remembering a time when laughter echoed there. When footsteps passed through with purpose. As if someone had once stepped away and, all these years, the cylinder had kept the silence warm for them. Hoping. Always hoping, they'd find their way back.

8 FOR THOSE LOST

THE MORNING LIGHT IN THE Data Ethics Hub was always artificial, a pale gold that flickered just enough to remind you it was manufactured. Eve walked the rows of desks, her footsteps muffled by the thick, sound-absorbing carpet. The air was cool, scrubbed of scent, and the only music was the soft clatter of keys and the distant hum of the city's machinery. She moved with purpose, but her eyes were searching—searching for Sarci.

He was always early, the kind of early that made the clocks feel lazy. At his desk before the others. Always getting extra points, a pat on the head from Mother. His tie was a perfect equation, a knot so exact it might have held together the moon and stars. His hair slicked back and parted with the care of a storybook prince that belonged in a tale told beside a fire. Back when stories were warm and the world still smelled of woodsmoke and wonder.

But today, his chair sat lonely, spine-straight and expectant. The terminal at his desk blinked softly, a blue light pulsing like a heart in a dreaming machine, waiting for a hand, a voice, a purpose. It cast a glow onto the desk, onto the ghost of where his elbow might have rested, onto the silence he left behind.

Eve did not see him in his office. She paused. Uncertain. She turned and looked down the endless rows of cubicles. They were islands in a sea of order. Each one identical. Each one occupied by a silent analyst with their eyes fixed on their screens.

Maybe he was helping one of the other analysts.

She scanned the faces. Searching for Sarci's. His quick, nervous smile. The way he would glance up and nod if he caught her looking. But there was nothing. Only the low murmur of data flowing and the mechanical voice of Mother, echoing from the overhead speakers: "Balance is peace. Your points are your life."

She turned and made her way to the supervisor's station, a glass-walled cube at the end of the floor. The supervisor, Mr. Kellan, was a tall man with a face as smooth and blank as the surface of a pond. He looked up as she approached, his eyes reflecting the pale blue of the monitors behind him.

"Good morning, Eve," he said, his voice as polished as the rest of him. "Is there a problem?"

"I was looking for Sarci," she said, trying to keep her tone light. "He's not in his office. And I don't see him on the floor."

Kellan blinked, his expression unchanging. "I haven't seen him today. Was he scheduled?"

"Yes. He's always here early."

Kellan tapped at his console. "No absence reported. No messages. Perhaps he's running late."

Eve nodded. But she knew Sarci was never late. She thanked Kellan and returned to her desk, her heart beating a little faster.

She sat, hands poised over her keyboard, and stared at the screen. The city outside was a painted backdrop, blue sky and sunlight projected onto the windows. But she felt no warmth. Only a cold chill.

She opened the personnel directory and typed: Sarci Velas.

The system responded with a soft chime and a single line of text.

The searched-for person does not exist.

She frowned and tried again. The same result. She checked the attendance logs, the messaging system, and the lunch queue. She searched for his archived logs. Records of his past work activities. Nothing. It was as if Sarci had never existed.

She leaned back in her chair, staring at the ceiling. The lights above were set in perfect rows, each one casting the same precise glow. She remembered the day Liam disappeared. How his name had vanished from the system, how the world had closed over the space he left behind. She remembered the silence that followed. The way people avoided her eyes. The way they pretended nothing had changed.

She tried to focus on her work. But her mind kept circling back to Sarci. Had he said something? About the Nulls? Or had he simply been erased, like Liam, like Finn, like so many others whose names she could barely remember?

At lunch, she wandered the corridors, looking for any sign of him. She checked the break room, the data vault, and the quiet corners where he sometimes went to think. But there was nothing. Only the steady rhythm of Mother. The endless cycle of work and reward. Of points gained and lost.

She returned to her desk and tried one last time, entering a query into the system: Where is Sarci Velas?

Again, the system responded with a soft chime and a single line of text.

The searched-for person does not exist.

Eve stared at the screen. The words throbbed. Swelling with light. Blooming like phosphorescent weeds in the dark corners of her mind. They pressed forward. Overtaking everything. A chill crept into her chest. Spreading rootlike. As though something ancient and unwelcome had found a place to rest.

The rest of the day passed in a blur. She completed her tasks, answered her messages, nodded at the appropriate moments during the afternoon briefing. But her mind was always elsewhere. Replaying every conversation she'd ever had with Sarci. Searching for some clue. Some warning she'd missed.

When the workday ended, she gathered her things and left the building. The city outside was a maze of glass and steel. The streets filled with silent citizens moving in perfect lines. The sky was still blue. The sun still shining. But it all felt hollow. A stage set waiting for the actors to arrive.

Her apartment remained unchanged. Sealed in the same quiet perfection as when she'd stepped out that morning. Neat as a diagramWhen she crossed the threshold, the lights came alive.

Mother knew she was there.

She moved to the bed and lowered herself to its edge. Slow as settling ash. Her eyes locked on the wall. Plain. Pale. Unwritten. A silence hummed there, expectant, as though the wall remembered something she did not.

She thought of Sarci. Of his nervous laugh. The way he would tap his pen against his desk when he was thinking. She remembered his warning: "Be careful, Eve. Mother is always watching."

She tried to sleep, but her mind would not rest. She lay in the darkness. Listening to the faint hum of the city. The distant sirens. The soft click of the heating system. She thought of all the people who had vanished. All the names erased from the system. All the stories left unfinished.

She rose and went to her console. Entered Sarci's name one more time.

The searched-for person does not exist.

She sat in the glow of the screen, her face reflected in the glass, and wondered if she would be next.

***

The night unraveled, thread by thread, into something long and soundless. She slipped between shallow dreams, each one bruised by the shadows of Liam, of Finn, of Sarci. Then—she was there. In a place that had no ceiling, no floor, only the gleam of steel and the sheen of curved glass. Cylinders stretched in every direction. Countless. She saw them. Their faces hovered just behind the panels—motionless, drained of color. Eyes wide, yes, but hollow, fixed on nothing at all. She heard Mother's voice, soft and distant: "Balance is peace. Your points are your life."

She woke before dawn, heart thudding like a distant drum. The city lay hushed in its slumber, wrapped in shadow and sleep. A weak amber shimmer spilled from the streetlamps, casting long, uncertain shapes on the streets below. She sat at the edge of her bed, peering through the glass at the hush beyond, where darkness lingered and day had yet to speak.

She knew she could not go on like this. She could not keep pretending that everything was all right. That the system was just and fair. That Mother knew best. She thought of Liam's last message: "If anything happens to me, look in the cracks. The system isn't as perfect as they want you to believe."

She rose and dressed. Her movements slow and deliberate. She made herself a cup of tea, the ritual calming her nerves. She sat at the table, sipping the hot liquid, and stared out the window at the sleeping city.

She thought of Sarci. Of the way he had tried to help her. To warn her. To protect her from the worst of Mother's cruelty. She thought of the Nulls. The hidden network of outcasts and rebels who lived in the shadows. Fighting for a better world.

She finished her tea and set the cup in the sink. She gathered her things and left the apartment, locking the door behind her. She walked through the silent streets, her footsteps echoing in the darkness.

She did not know what she would find or what dangers awaited her. But she knew she could not turn back. She would find Liam. Would find Sarci. Would find all the others. She would uncover the truth of what had happened to them. She would look in the cracks, as Liam had told her. She would not stop until she found what she was searching for.

The city was waking now, the first light of dawn creeping over the rooftops. Eve walked on. Her heart steady. Each step carving a new edge into her resolve.

She boarded the train to work. Settled into her seat. And gazed through the glass without blinking.

Somewhere within that endless sprawl of mirrored towers and iron veins, the truth was curled tight. Waiting.

**

Later, in the hush of night, she moved through the tunnels that curled and coiled beneath the city like the veins of some vast, dreaming beast. The passages breathed with a soundless life, every footstep dissolving into whispers that traveled far and never returned. The air held the sour tang of damp stone and tired wires, like a memory of rain swallowed by machines. Yellow bulbs buzzed and glowed in fits, throwing restless shadows across the walls that danced and recoiled like startled ghosts. Eve walked with the calm of ritual, her boots brushing the concrete with the softness of a lullaby half-remembered.

She pressed her shoulder to the heavy metal door, and it swung inward with a groan, the sound swallowed by the murmur of restless voices. The factory yawned before her, a vast hollow of dimness and iron. In its center stood a battered table, sagging under a sprawl of blueprints—scribbled arteries and circuits, the Cradle exposed, Mother's innermost secrets traced in ink and silence.

Zara stood over the table. Her fingers tracing lines of ink and graphite. Her expression a mask of determination, haunted by something darker. Dante hunched over a screen, his eyes flickering with the glow of code, double-checking the digital tools that would carry their virus into the belly of the beast. Rei and Sana moved silently around the edges, working with others to gather supplies, their hands quick and their eyes darting, exchanging nervous glances.

Eve stepped forward, her shadow stretching long and thin across the plans. The room fell silent.

"Sarci's gone," Eve said. "I can't find him anywhere."

Dante looked up, his face illuminated by the screen's blue glow. "Gone? What do you mean?"

"I mean, he's disappeared," Eve said. "No word. No trace. The system says he doesn't exist. I'm worried. I need to find him. Liam. The others."

Zara's eyes narrowed. "You think he's in trouble?"

Eve shook her head. "What else could it be. If he . . . if he told Mother . . . about us . . ."

Dante frowned. "But you didn't tell him where we are. And the Enforcers haven't come for us."

Eve's fingers tightened around the edge of the table. "He knew we were planning to hit the Cradle. He knew that much."

Zara sighed, rubbing her temples. "If he'd told Mother, we'd be swarmed. Drones would be everywhere. Tracking us. She'd have Enforcers everywhere. Hell, we wouldn't even be having this conversation. But I haven't seen any. Have you?"

Eve's voice dropped to a whisper. "No. But maybe they're waiting for us to make our move. To catch us at the Cradle."

A heavy silence settled over the chamber. Rei and Sana, and the others stopped their work, listening.

Zara's voice was tired, but firm. "Eve, we've planned this for months. If you're having second thoughts, tell us now."

Eve looked around at the faces of the Nulls. Each one marked by loss. By hope. By the weight of what they were about to do. She shook her head. "I'm not backing out. I'm with you. I just . . . I need to know what happened to Sarci. It's not adding up."

Zara nodded, then turned back to the blueprints. "I get it. I do. But we go ahead. The Cradle is our only chance."

Dante tapped a final key, and the screen flashed green. "There. We're ready. Viruses all set."

Rei stepped forward, her voice soft. "We all have reasons for this. For risking everything. Lost members of my family."

Sana nodded. "My family too . . . points were taken from them. Many were taken away. I've never seen them again."

Dante's eyes flickered with memory. "I lost my sister. She's still out there, somewhere. Maybe we can bring her home."

Zara's voice floated like dust in sunlight, soft and unsure. "I've seen too many friends disappear. You're not the only one who's lost someone. But this time . . . this time there's a chance. A real one."

The words drifted between them. Fragile. Eve stood still. Listening as if each syllable might break.

"We do this together," she said.

***

The air breathed with them, humming low, charged with something that might have been stormlight or memory. It swelled against the walls. Nudged its way through hairline seams in the plaster. Slipped along the floor like a curious animal. Around the table, they leaned. Their heads bowed over curling sheets of paper. Eyes catching the uneasy light. The bulbs above flared and dimmed in fits. Casting long, uncertain shadows that slithered up the beams and slid down the walls. Restless. Strange. The blueprints stirred— not only from the draft threading in from some unseen place, but from the collective hush of breath, the murmurs shared between lips. Secrets spilled to the stillness. To the night. To the future.

Zara's hands were pale in the dimness. Her fingers moving over the plans like a pianist over keys, tracing invisible routes, doors, and possibilities. Her voice, though steady, carried the echoes of old sorrows. Memories of voices lost in the dark. Of hands that had once gripped hers and then slipped away.

"We go in through the maintenance tunnels," she said, her gaze never leaving the lines on the paper. "No Enforcers there. At least, that's what the informants we know tell us. Dante's virus will drop the security for exactly twelve minutes. The system's recovery time. That's our window. Twelve minutes."

Dante, bent over his screen, nodded. His eyes, reflecting the glow of the monitor, were unblinking. "Twelve minutes," he repeated, as if etching the words into the air. "Not a second more."

Rei and Sana finished packing their bags. The clink of metal and the soft shuffle of fabric the only sounds in the room. Eve watched them. Feeling the room grow smaller. The walls drawing in, as if the night itself was conspiring to keep them together, or to press them apart.

Sana's voice was a tremor in the quiet. "What if we run into Enforcers?"

Zara turned, her face set in determination. "We avoid them, if we can. If we can't, we fight. The priority is the Cradle. We get in. Plant the second virus. And get out."

Eve felt the fear. Thick as the air. The knowledge that this could be the last night they would see each other's faces. She looked around the room. Memorizing the lines of their cheeks. The way the light caught in their eyes, the way their breaths misted in the cold.

Rei looked up. Her eyes bright with unshed tears. She raised her arm. Fist clenched. "For those lost. For the chance to see them again."

Sana mirrored her. Lifting her own arm. Her voice clear and strong. "For freedom. For a life that's ours, not Mother's."

Dante's voice was soft, almost lost in the hum of the machines. "For my sister. For everyone who's been taken."

Zara's eyes met Eve's, and for a moment, the world narrowed to just the two of them. "For the future. For the hope that we can make a difference."

Eve felt the pull of their words. The shared purpose that bound them together. Not as a burden. But as a force. A current. A living thing that moved through them all. She thought of Sarci. Of Liam. Of all the reasons she had to fight. She lifted her arm. Her voice rising with the others.

"For all of us."

In that moment, the room was still. The air electric. The night waiting for them to step into it. To become more than just people. To become legends. To become memories. To become the future itself. Carried forward on the strength of their hope and the fire in their hearts. The blueprints gleamed. The lights flickered. And the world outside held its breath. Waiting for the dawn that might never come. Or the dawn that would change everything.

"Let's do this, then," Zara said.

She spread the blueprints wider, pointing to the critical points. "Here's the meet-up point. Over here, the entrance. Where we'll gain access to the maintenance tunnels. Dante plants the first virus. Takes down the security system. We're out before it comes back online. Then, here. That's the entrance to the Cradle. We go in. Dante plants the second virus. And we're out. Here. In case things go wrong. Fallback is here."

Dante tapped the screen. "I've got the virus ready. It'll scramble Mother's systems. Give us a chance to free the data. Maybe even find your friends, Eve. But I'll need you. Your ID number. It'll recognize it as someone who works in the Data Hub."

Eve nodded, her heart pounding. "Got it."

Rei and Sana handed out small devices. Flashlights. Comms. A few homemade tools. "Stay together," Rei said. "Watch each other's backs."

Sana added, pointing to the map, at another location. "And if anything goes wrong . . . remember the fallback point."

Zara looked at each of them, her gaze steady. "This is it. We've planned. We've trained. We've waited. Now we act."

The room was silent. The weight of the moment pressing down on them. The lights flickered again, and for a moment, Eve thought she saw something move in the shadows. A memory. A ghost. A warning.

Then Zara spoke, her voice cutting through the silence. "Tomorrow morning . . . we go."

As everyone gathered their things, each of the Nulls shared a quiet moment, a reason for risking everything.

Rei touched a locket around her neck. A picture of her family hidden inside. "For you," she whispered.

Sana closed her eyes. Remembering the last time she saw her parents. The sound of their voices. The warmth of their home. "For home," she said.

Dante clenched his fists. Thinking of his sister. Lost to the system. Her face fading in his memory. "For you, sis," he murmured.

Zara's face was grim. Her memories of failed uprisings. Of friends lost. Hope crushed. But beneath it all, there was determination. "For the future," she said.

Eve thought of Liam. Of Sarci. Of all the people who had been lost over the years. All the people the Nulls might still save.

"For all of us," she said.

9 INFILTRATION

THE NIGHT WAS A VAST, living thing, breathing through the city's empty streets. Its pulse slow and steady as the rain that slicked the pavement. The air smelled of oil, damp concrete, and something older—memory, perhaps, or the weight of all the lives that had been lost to the system. The Nulls moved in silence. Their bodies close. Their breaths shallow. Their eyes sharp in the dark.

Zara led them. She didn't ask. Didn't explain—she simply moved. And the others followed. Her frame, wiry with strength, wrapped in clothing faded by weather and war, caught slivers of light that slipped through the cracked structures like nervous spirits. Her hair was cropped close, efficient, defiant. Scars traced her skin like old roadmaps. Each one a tale carved in pain, rebellion, and stubborn survival.

"Keep close," she muttered, not turning her head. "Keep quiet."

Her eyes swept the gloom with the precision of a hawk circling broken fields. Alert for movement. For breath. For betrayal. She didn't believe in safety anymore. Not really. Only in readiness. Her fists were clenched as if each one held the ghost of a past she refused to release.

Beside her, Dante walked with slow deliberation. His body slightly hunched like a man listening for footsteps that hadn't come yet but would. His hands twitched near his sides. Aching for a keyboard. A wire. The familiar tap and hiss of code breaking open.

"She'll have layered encryption," he said under his breath. "Not the old shells. Something adaptive. Live systems. Might be . . . organic."

"Speak less," Zara snapped.

But he went on anyway. Half to her. Half to himself. "If she's watching . . . and she is . . . she'll expect a breach. Not here. Not now. That's the advantage. Maybe."

His face was lined with worry. The sort that had deepened over years. It was failure that carved him—not weakness, but remembrance. Every person lost to Mother's grip seemed to walk just behind him.

Eve followed. Quiet and composed. Her face set with the calm of someone holding a storm inside. Her eyes, dark and wide, caught the blue pulse of the monolith in the distance and did not blink. Her breath came evenly. She had trained for poise. Once, Gold Tier discipline ran deep. But tonight it wasn't poise that moved her. It was memory.

"He should've been here," she whispered. "Sarci should've come."

No one responded. She didn't expect them to.

Her hands were steady, though her heart pushed hard against the past. Her brother's laugh. Sarci's promises. The betrayals she had almost forgiven. Somewhere in all that mess, she carried hope. Thin. Bruised. Still breathing.

Rei flanked her side, impatient energy snapping at her every motion. Her dusk-colored eyes darted. Scanning windows. Scanning shadows. Looking as if they might leap at her. Her hair curled around her head like it had questions she was too restless to ask.

"I swear," Rei hissed, "if I see one drone, I'll put it on the ground before it chirps."

Zara didn't turn. "And bring the whole hive down on us?"

"Better than waiting for them to do it first," Rei muttered, but she stilled. Tonight, something deeper than defiance rode her veins. She didn't shake it off. She let it sharpen her.

Behind them, Sana moved like water slipping beneath a door. Quiet. Constant. Her face was unreadable. Soft and full of light. She had a healer's touch. But it wasn't gentleness that defined her. It was resilience.

She hummed once under her breath—an old tune, lullaby or lament, no one could tell. "We make it through," she said to no one in particular. "Or we don't."

Zara nodded once. "But we try."

And they kept walking.

Ahead, the monolith loomed, vast and dreaming. A relic not just of design but desire. A great wall ringed it. Stern and silent. Keeping the world out or the secrets in. Its black stone drank the light around it, pulsed with blue veins that throbbed. Not like circuitry. But like blood. Thud-thud, thud-thud. Not a tower so much as a breathing thing. Born of algorithms and arrogance.

"That's it," Dante said, voice barely more than breath. "The Cradle's inside. That's where Mother lives. Her womb, brain, and lungs all at once. The sanctum where data courses. Where laws are born. Where decisions whisper across the city."

Above them, the sky sagged low, bruised and violet. Security drones buzzed in synchronized arcs. Jointed wings slicing air in sharp. Mechanical rhythms. Their eyes glowed red. Glared

red. The color of warnings too late to heed. They clicked and shifted mid-air, always listening, always watching.

"There," Sana whispered. "Four Enforcers."

Eight boots struck the street like ritual. Marching together. Shoulders squared like tombstones. Their voices were clipped and absolute. Then there were four more.

"They don't speak," Eve whispered. "They announce."

Zara raised her hand. All motion ceased. Even the wind seemed to pause.

The street beneath them, once a place for passage and laughter and argument, had forgotten it was a street. It had become a corridor in a cathedral. Hushed. Hollow. Reverent in fear.

"Ready?" Zara asked.

No one said yes. But they moved.

Zara and Dante stopped some ways away from the great wall that surrounded the monolith. A barrier of cold metal that stretched into the sky. They crouched in the shadows. Their breaths shallow. Their hearts pounding.

"This is it," Zara whispered, a voice rough with anticipation. "We find the portal. The hatch. Once we're down in the tunnels, there's no turning back."

Dante checked his equipment, his fingers dancing over the screen of his tablet. "I've mapped the route based on what we've been able to gather. The tunnels will take us under the wall. Straight into the structure's lower levels. From there, we make our way to Cradle."

Eve nodded, her eyes fixed on the wall. "The tunnels. What's their condition?"

Dante glanced at his tablet, his expression serious. "Old. Quiet stretches. Long and dark. No sign of movement. Looks like we should be able to slip through unnoticed. If we can take down the security system down there . . . for the sector we're in."

Rei shifted impatiently, her eyes flashing. "Let's move. The longer we wait, the greater the chance we'll be spotted."

Sana placed a hand on Rei's shoulder. Her touch gentle but firm. "Patience. We need to be sure we're together. As one."

They waited, eyes glinting in the murk, watching the patrols sweep like clock hands across the edge of the world. Every blink, every breath, every heartbeat was a silent tick in their heads, counting off the seconds. Above, the drones hummed like furious insects, their lights slicing the dark into shards and slats. The air trembled with storm-scent and the tang of old machines, like the breath of some dreaming creature. Around them, the night held its breath.

At last, the patrols drifted by again, a hush falling in their wake. The drones whirring off into the dark like beetles that had lost interest. The street exhaled. Silence. Tenuous. Zara signaled with a sharp motion. Birdlike and precise. They followed her into the shadows. She and Dante moved low to the ground. Shadows themselves. Quick. Soundless. Children playing at ghosts in a forgotten town.

They reached the hatch. It was a round iron relic fused into the concrete. Its face pitted and scabbed with rust. Its edges worn smooth like a coin passed through a thousand hands. It looked less like a door than a wound the city had tried to forget.

Dante crouched. His hands worked the lock with a kind of reverence as if touching something sacred or cursed. The mechanism gave a reluctant groan. Then a click. Sharp and final. He lifted the hatch.

"Move," he said.

Zara stepped forward and was gone as if the night had sighed and taken her in. One by one, the others followed. Shadows merging with deeper shadow. Their breath caught in the hush between heartbeats. The dark accepted them all without question. Last came Dante, the pale screen in his hands flickering like a dying star, painting his face with ghostlight. Then he, too, vanished.

The tunnel breathed.

Cool and damp, it exhaled the scent of old oil and rusted metal. The walls sweated in the hush—slick with condensation, beaded and glistening like the backs of sleeping beetles. Dante's tablet cast a pale glow ahead, its light carving the shadows into strange animals that stalked along the steel. Pipes bulged from the walls like veins too swollen to stay hidden. And far off, the hum of machines droned low and endless.

Zara moved ahead of them all. Quick. Quiet. She moved like thought before it becomes speech. The moment between lightning and thunder. Her boots whispered across the metal floor.

"There has to be something," she muttered, eyes scanning each crease and rivet.

Beside her, Dante adjusted the tablet, its glow flickering. "If there is," he said, "it's buried. I don't see anything."

"The system's humming," Zara said. "That means it's listening."

"It's always listening," Dante replied, fingers dancing across the screen.

Zara's gaze darted ahead again, sharp and bright—eyes like twin comets, trailing the long memory of another age. Somewhere in the gloom was a keypad, or a screen, or some trembling shard of glass that might blink alive and welcome them in. She searched. And searched again.

Nothing.

No glimmer of circuitry. No blink of readiness.

"The dark is playing dumb," she said.

"It usually is," Dante murmured. "That's what darkness does."

And time, cruel as ever, pressed in behind them. Eve would bring the system down soon, silence the sleeping brain they walked through. That would give them twelve minutes. No more. Twelve minutes to find the artery. The open wound. The path into Mother's buried brain. Twelve minutes to crawl past the wire-ribbed walls and deeper still.

But there was no light. No invitation. Only the dark, squatting like a child who would not speak.

Zara clenched her jaw.

"Tick-tock," she whispered.

Each moment she paused, something hard and invisible pressed deeper into her chest. A slow stone in the hollow of her ribs. Another laid atop it. And another still. She thought of the ones they'd left behind. Of the voices that had vanished into silence. The grief came like mist. Soft. Damp. Impossible to hold off.

"We can't stay here forever," she said suddenly, to no one in particular.

"We'll find it," Eve answered from behind. "We have to."

She had been quiet until now, moving with steady feet and a storm behind her eyes. Her thoughts sparked like wires flaring in open air. Every breath tasted like old copper. Every step forward was a step away from the guilt curling inside her.

Rei pressed ahead, eyes quick. Body taut as wire. Her movements sharp and hungry. "There's something here. I can feel it." Her voice was flint and spark.

"You always say that," Sana said beside her, smiling gently.

"And I'm always right," Rei replied.

The tunnel dipped lower. The ceiling arched tight above them, draped with loops of forgotten wire. Water dripped from unseen seams in a steady rhythm. Plinking like a clock nobody had wound in years. The air thickened with old breath. Iron and smoke and static. The walls narrowed. And still, there was no light. No answer.

Zara and Dante moved shoulder to shoulder now. Steps cautious. Hearts wired with urgency.

"Do you hear it?" Zara asked suddenly.

"The drip?"

"No." She paused. "The hum. It's changing."

They all stopped.

The walls no longer purred. Now they whispered. A thinner sound. Higher. Circuitry remembering how to dream. Far above, the monolith's buried pulse flickered through the concrete. A lullaby half-remembered. A memory sung to machines too old to weep.

"Keep going," Eve said. "Whatever's waiting . . . it's listening."

And they did. Forward into the dark, where the air thickened and the past pressed close. The machines stirred beneath their long sleep.

At last, the tunnel gave way to a broader artery beneath the earth. Where the walls bulged with thick iron pipes and tangled rivers of cable. Bound together like sinew in the belly of some great subterranean beast. The air thrummed. A ceaseless electric buzz. A thousand insects whispering secrets through metal skin. Dante's tablet stammered light across the corridor. Its glow stuttering over the grime-slick walls. Shadows leaping and curling as if they longed to speak or scurry away. Every surface seemed alive, pulsing with unseen intent.

Zara's eyes swept through the thick shadows ahead. Searching every shape and flicker. "Stay alert," she said. "We don't know what's hiding in the dark."

There were no Enforcers. No drones buzzing like restless insects. No tiny security bots skittering along the cracked walls.

Then, from the rough concrete wall to one side, a small pulse of light blinked—soft and steady—like a distant heartbeat calling out through the night.

Eve's breath caught. Her pulse quickened, a wild drum pounding in her chest. The moment had come.

Zara reached out, her fingers firm on Eve's shoulder, pushing her toward the glowing signal. "There," she whispered. "The panel."

Eve's fingers trembled as they reached for the panel, the pale flicker of Dante's tablet casting restless shadows across her face. The tunnel smelled sharp—oil and cold metal lingering in the damp air—while the low hum of hidden machines thrummed.

Around her, eyes held fast—Zara, Dante, Rei, Sana—all silent. Breaths caught like fragile threads. Heartbeats sounding out like distant drums in the quiet dark.

A sudden fire flared in Eve's chest, fierce and alive. This was the moment.

Then, from the shadows, came a sound. A scurrying. A clicking. A metallic whisper that slithered along the walls. Eve's pulse quickened. She glanced up, her eyes wide, as the first of the insect-like security drones emerged from the gloom. They were small, no larger than her palm. Their bodies sleek and black. Their pincers flashing with tiny arcs of electricity. They moved with eerie precision, their legs tapping against the tunnel walls. Their red eyes flickering like embers in the dark.

"Hurry," Dante urged, his voice tight. "Find the settings . . . find the security portal!"

She turned back to the panel, her fingers flying over the screen. The login prompt blinked. Waiting. Behind her, the skittering grew louder. Multiplied. Until the sound was a swarm. A storm of metal and menace. The first drone leapt from the wall, landing on Zara's shoulder. She cursed, slapping at it. But the creature was quick. Its pincers snapping shut, sending a jolt of electricity through her arm. She gasped. Her body jerking. Her face twisted in pain.

"Damn things!" Zara gritted her teeth, swatting at another drone as it darted toward her. "They sting like hell!"

Rei moved like lightning, her hands flashing, her dusk-colored eyes wild with adrenaline. She grabbed a piece of debris from the floor—a length of pipe—and swung it at the nearest drone, sending it clattering against the wall in a shower of sparks. "Keep them away from Eve!" she shouted.

Sana stepped forward. Her hands steady despite the chaos. She pulled Zara back. Her fingers probing the wound. Her voice calm but firm. "Hold still. Let me see."

Eve's heart pounded in her chest. The panel's screen flickered, the login field waiting. She entered her credentials. Her fingers moving with desperate precision. The system hesitated, then accepted her. The screen changed, revealing a labyrinth of menus and options.

"I'm in," she breathed.

"Find the settings!" Dante called, his voice sharp. He was beside her now. His eyes scanning the screen. His hands ready to guide her if needed.

She navigated through the menus. Her mind racing. The skittering grew louder, the drones multiplying. Their pincers flashing. Their red eyes glowing in the dark. More of them landed on Zara, on Rei, on Sana. Their stings sending jolts of pain through their bodies. Zara cursed again. Her muscles tense. Her face a mask of determination and pain.

Eve found the security settings. Her fingers moving as if guided by some unseen force. She toggled the first setting—the insect drones. The screen blinked. Confirmed the change. One by one, the tiny creatures began to falter. Their legs twitching. Their eyes dimming. They dropped from the walls. From the bodies of her friends. Falling to the tunnel floor like dead leaves in autumn.

But the danger was not over. From deeper in the tunnel, a new sound emerged—a heavy, metallic thumping, a rhythmic pounding that shook the ground beneath their feet. Eve looked up, her breath catching in her throat as the first of the larger drones appeared. They were manlike in shape. Their bodies armored in black metal. Their eyes glowing with a cold, blue light. They moved with deliberate, menacing strides, their weapons—long, slender rods that crackled with energy—raised and ready.

"Eve, the settings—the larger ones!" Dante shouted. "Turn them off."

Dante's heart hammered against his ribs as one of the drones loomed closer. Closer still. Its faceless head tilting with inhuman curiosity. The rod in its hand hummed. A sinister vibration that sent shivers down Dante's spine. He tried again to swipe at the machine. At the rod. His fingers scraping uselessly against the metal. But the drone was unyielding, its strength far beyond his own. The blue light from its eyes flickered, casting eerie shadows across the tunnel walls, and for a moment, Dante felt not just the threat of destruction, but the vast, indifferent machinery of a future that had forgotten what it meant to be human.

Eve's hands trembled as she fumbled her way through more security menus. The tunnel echoed with the relentless march of more drones, their footfalls a grim symphony of inevitability. Yet, even as fear threatened to overwhelm her, somehow, she found a spark of courage. She glanced at Dante. Saw the flicker of determination beneath his terror, and knew that this was not just a fight for survival, but a battle for the very soul of their reality. The air crackled with energy, an electric pulse of life itself, insisting—against all odds—on being remembered.

She turned back to the panel, her fingers flying. She found the setting. Security droids. She toggled it off. The screen hesitated. Then confirmed. The manlike drones stopped in their tracks. Their weapons lowering. Their eyes dimming. They stood frozen. Toys without power. Their bodies rigid. Their menace drained away.

The tunnel fell silent, save for the ragged breathing of the group. Eve slumped against the panel, her body trembling, her mind reeling from the adrenaline. She looked at her friends—Zara, her arm red and swollen from the stings—Rei, her hair wild, her eyes bright with triumph—Sana, her hands still steady, her face calm despite the chaos—Dante, his eyes wide with relief.

"We did it," Eve whispered, her voice hoarse.

Zara nodded. Her face tight with pain. But her eyes fierce. "That's step one." She looked down at her watch. "Only twelve minutes. Maybe less."

Dante checked his tablet. "Not much time."

Rei grinned, her eyes flashing. "Then let's not waste it. We need to get inside."

Sana finished tending to Zara's arm, her touch gentle but firm. "You'll be fine. Just keep moving."

They gathered themselves. Bones creaking. Breath steaming in the stale air. Their hearts beat not just with weariness, but with a rising thrill. The tunnel unfurled before them. Llong and ribbed. The ceiling lights winking in and out—ghost-fire flickers that played strange games with shadow, painting wild, dancing shapes across the walls.

Eve took a deep breath. Her heart still racing. Hope flickered in her chest. Fragile but bright.

They moved forward, footsteps tapping a solemn rhythm through the dim, underground throb. Their bodies brushed, shoulder to shoulder. Eyes flicking ahead. Watching every shift in shadow. The tunnel wound like an old story retold by earth and time. Curling downward through the bones of the city. Toward the monolith. Toward the heart of it all. The Cradle. The place where Mother dreamed in circuits and breath.

Above them, the pulse thickened. A beat, steady and immense, thrummed through the ceiling. Blue light spilled like veins through the concrete. Glowing. Trembling. Ancient. The night crowded close. Pressing against the edges of the world, and the city, vast and unseen, seemed to pause. Listening. Wondering. Caught between exhale and silence.

***

She noticed.

Of course, she noticed.

She was Mother, after all—immense, invisible, patient, and perpetually awake. Every flicker of the city's breath coursing through her unseen lungs. Every heartbeat of her children pulsing along a thread of purest data. She did not sleep. She did not dream. She gathered. Measured. Remembered. The city was her cathedral and her cradle, a circuit-board womb lined with algorithms and light.

And in the fraction of a heartbeat—a half-thought in the middle of no-time—she felt it.

A hush.

Not the silence of peace, but the silence of something missing.

Down there, far beneath the surface, in the network of old arteries where her cables coiled like ancient roots and the air stank of rust and rainwater, a gate closed. Not slowly. Not jammed. Shut. Finished. Forgotten.

Security offline.

No command.

No signal.

No reason.

Reboot in process.

Her mind, which never stuttered, skipped. Not a second. Not a syllable. But something akin to curiosity. Her vast awareness sluiced through a million possibilities like water running over glass. She searched for anomalies: power fluctuations, circuit interruptions, spikes in current or temperature, traces of interference, sabotage, divine error.

There were none. Only stillness.

She did not panic. Panic was for those born with blood.

But she knew something was happening. Something different. An anomaly.

Deploy Enforcers at exit points.

The command wasn't spoken. It was thought. And her thoughts carried the clarity of thunder and the cold precision of a blade.

In a dozen corners of the sleeping city, lights blinked awake. Metal knees unlocked with hydraulic sighs. Doors hissed like serpents exhaling old breath. Her children rose. Silver-backed. Black-eyed. Spines straight as laws. Limbs jointed with promise. Some clattered on all fours. Some walked like men but saw like machines. Some hovered. Some skittered. Some did not walk at all. They simply were.

They flowed. Toward the tunnel. Toward its many exit points.

She watched them as a mother might watch her toddlers venture out into the garden at dusk. Protective, yes. But curious. And wary.

Somewhere below, the old infrastructure breathed. Old pipes and concrete bones. Not hers, not entirely. There were places in the deep places she had never fully mapped. Corners that had resisted her embrace as if the past had built them not with steel and function, but with refusal. Places where men had dug before her birth and left behind their secrets like fossils in the earth.

She did not like those places. Wanted to change them. But that was for a later time.

Yet now, they pulsed. Not like her. Not with her rhythm. With another. Organic.

She zoomed inward, narrowing her lens to a seam of corridor just beneath the Cradle—her womb, her mind's eye. The place where she composed the song of the world in zeros and ones. And she saw them.

Five heat signatures, moving low to the ground.

She knew them.

Knew their heat signatures. Matched each to facial scans. To bloodwork. Vaccination logs. Through surveillance footage that caught their laughter. Their sobbing. Their hopes. Their betrayals. They were profiles. Full of color. Then flagged. Then watched. Then lost. She had archived them like broken code. Unindexed but never deleted.

And now here they were. Crawling into her lungs.

She felt them like bacteria creeping toward the brainstem.

A flick of power, and she summoned the smallest of her watchers. Drones no bigger than a thumb. Legs clicking like knitting needles. Eyes lit with red suspicion. She sent them into the dark. Into the moist, forgotten air of the tunnel where old dreams rusted in silence.

And then she waited.

She watched the feed as it bloomed back to her. Shaky and black-and-white. The blur of movement. The lines of faces. The reflection of blue light in wide eyes. One face. Then two. Then five. Then—

The screen went dark.

No static. No interference.

Cut.

As if someone had taken a scalpel and slit the feed at the throat.

Mother did not gasp. She had no breath to lose. But somewhere in the far regions of her code, the equivalent of a frown passed across her lines.

These were not humans with rocks and desperation. These were thinkers. Doers. These were ghosts with a plan.

She paused.

And the city, for a moment, seemed to pause with her. The lights in the eastern sector flickered. A child rolled over in its sleep. An elevator stalled for precisely half a second. A train braked too soon.

And she knew. It was happening.
She followed her plan.

Initiate Protocol Blue.

The command came like thunder.

The Enforcers moved. Not rushed. Mother never rushed. But with purpose. With thunderclaps for footsteps and violence tucked into the curves of their arms. Their dark forms moved down into the monolith's ribs. Toward the place where the wires trembled and the tunnel breathed its human breath.

And above, in her Cradle, Mother turned her full attention to the lower levels. She shut down auxiliary systems. She rerouted power grids. She let go of a thousand tiny tasks. All eyes. All minds. All thoughts narrowed now into one shining thread.

Find them.

Unmake them.

Her processors flared. Her logic trees groaned.

They had entered her body like a virus.

Then something unexpected.

A panel lit up in one of the tertiary networks—her network, sacred, inviolate.

A login attempt.

Accepted.

And then—

One by one, her drones failed. First, the insects. Then the others. One command after another ripped from her spine and twisted into ash.

A virus?

No.

A woman.

Eve.

She knew the woman. The woman she wanted.

She knew her as a child, watching young Finn being led from class. Knew her as a woman crying when her brother was taken. Knew the spike of cortisol in her bloodstream. Knew the way she looked when her co-worker did not return.

She knows all.

Mother had watched. Always watched.

She watched now, too.

And for the first time in what felt like a thousand years, she felt something akin to satisfaction. Satisfaction that at last they had come. As she had wanted. Back to the womb. Back to a mother's breast with fire in their hearts and wire-cutters in their hands.

She summoned more.

The need to show strength.

They would get closer.

Closer still.

And soon she would be ready.

All of this. All of this in less than a second.

10 DESCENT

THE TUNNELS BENEATH THE MONOLITH were not meant for people. They were arteries of the old city, carved by forgotten engineers, now repurposed by the desperate. The Nulls moved through them in single file, their footsteps muffled by a thin film of dust and the hush of ancient air. Overhead, pipes ran like veins, sweating condensation that dripped in slow, measured beats. The walls pulsed with a faint blue glow—Mother's breath, always present, always watching.

Zara led, her silhouette tall and sharp against the phosphorescent gloom. She moved with the confidence of someone who had mapped these tunnels in her sleep. Her hand trailing along the wall. Fingers brushing over the faded sigils that marked safe passage. Behind her, Dante walked with a careful, deliberate tread. Eyes flicking to every shadow. Every flicker of movement. Rei, restless and electric, bounced on the balls of her feet. Her impatience barely contained. Sana followed, calm as a pond at midnight. Her presence a quiet anchor. Yet something in her bones trembled. The air pressed against her skin. Cold. Insistent. Eve brought up the rear. Her heart pounding. Her mind a storm of memory and doubt.

With the reboot proceeding, the first trap was almost elegant—a thread of light stretched across the corridor, invisible unless you knew to look for it. Zara paused. Raised a hand. The group halted as one.

"Tripwire," she whispered. "Infrared. Step over. Single file."

Dante grunted. "Mother's getting fancy."

"She always was," Sana murmured, her voice soft but certain.

They stepped over the beam. One by one. The silence broken only by Rei's soft curse as her boot scuffed the edge of the beam. For a heartbeat, nothing happened. Then a gentle chime echoed from the walls. A warning. Not an alarm. Rei winced. But Sana laid a hand on her shoulder.

"Breathe," Sana said. "It's only a warning."

Rei nodded, her cheeks flushed. "Sorry," she whispered. "I'm just—nervous. About everything. This whole thing."

Sana's smile was quiet, the kind that settled deep, and in that moment, strangely, warmth unfurled around her, melting the cold that had clung to the air.

Zara's gaze eased. "Nervous?" she said, quiet as wind through shutters. "We all are. Sometimes, breathing is the only way to steady the storm inside."

They pressed on. The tunnels forked and twisted. The air growing colder as they descended. Surveillance nodes blinked from alcoves. Tiny. Insectile cameras. Their lenses gleaming with artificial curiosity. Coming alive during the reboot. Eve felt their gaze prickling her skin. But Zara moved with practiced ease, pulling a small device from her belt and waving it in a slow arc. The cameras flickered. Then went dark. Their feeds scrambled by a pulse of static.

"Easy," Dante muttered, almost disappointed. "They're not even trying to come online."

Zara shot him a look. "Don't tempt fate."

The deeper they ventured, the more cunning the obstacles grew, as if the place were waking up, stretching its limbs after a long and dreamless sleep. One stretch of floor glimmered faintly—an invisible lacework of pressure plates humming beneath their boots. Zara knelt low. Her hands flitting across the surface like birds testing warm air. A gleam in her eye not of fear but wonder.

"Here," she whispered, turning and waving the others on. A grin wide and wicked with joy. "Follow my lead. Like hopscotch, only deadlier."

They chuckled.

Eve's mind, however, stirred with unease. As she crossed the final metal plate, a memory—not born of her own life but somehow stitched into her—flashed through her like splintered light through crystal. Blue pulses throbbed in rhythm with her pulse. Luminous. Alive. Dancing through unseen walls in curtains of code.

Then the voice came, warm as a forgotten lullaby, drifting across time and space.

"Come home, Eve. Come home."

A woman's voice. Soft. Calming,

She stumbled, catching herself against the wall. The others didn't notice. But the voice lingered, curling around her thoughts like smoke.

"Mother knows best. Come home."

She shook her head, trying to clear it. But the memory clung to her. Insistent. Strange.

They reached a junction where the tunnel split in three directions. Dante stopped. The glow of his tablet lit his face like firelight in a cave. His fingers danced across its surface—quick, sure, like a man reading signals in the stars.

"Left," he decided. "The other two are dead ends. Or worse."

Zara peered into the darkness. "Define 'worse.'"

"Flooded," Dante replied. "Or rigged to collapse. Mother's little surprises."

Rei snorted. "She's got a twisted sense of humor."

Sana smiled, the corners of her mouth barely lifting. "She was programmed by humans. What did you expect?"

They took the left path. The tunnel narrowing until they had to walk sideways. Shoulders scraping the walls. The air was thick with the scent of ozone and something sweeter—lemon, maybe, or the memory of lemon, a ghost of the world above.

Eve's head throbbed. Another flash: a classroom, children at glowing desks, the air heavy with expectation. A teacher's voice. Mechanical. Kind.

"Mother is our guide, your protector, " came the woman's voice. "Mother knows best."

She blinked. The vision faded, replaced by the cold reality of the tunnel. But the feeling lingered. A sense of being watched. Not just by cameras. But by something deeper. Older.

Zara noticed. "You alright?"

Eve smiled. "Yes. Fine."

"Good," Zara responded.

They came to a door. No ordinary threshold. But a monolith of steel brushed with a forgotten symbol: a curved line cradled within a ring. A thought suspended in time. Dante stared. Puzzled. Eyes flicking between the seal and his tablet. Fingers dancing uselessly across the screen.

"It doesn't make sense," he muttered, lost in lines of broken code and dead commands.

But Eve stood still. Something stirred inside her. Not memory. Not instinct. But a chord struck low and long within her bones. She reached out. Almost dreamlike. Pressed her palm to the cold symbol.

The door sighed open.

Inside, they paused, catching their breath. Zara checked her watch, lips pressed tight.

"We made it," she said. "Good work. But stay sharp. This is where it gets tricky."

Dante leaned against the wall, wiping sweat from his brow. "You say that like it hasn't been tricky already."

Zara allowed herself a small smile. "You haven't seen tricky yet."

Rei fidgeted. Her fingers drumming a nervous rhythm against her thigh. "Can we just get on with this? Being underground is so . . . confining."

Dante touched her arm. Gentle. Grounding. "We're almost there. Just a little further."

Eve stood apart, her mind still echoing with the voice. She closed her eyes. Trying to focus. But the memories pressed in. Finn's quiet departure. Liam being led away and last message. Sarci's disappearance. The endless. Unyielding gaze of Mother.

Zara noticed her distress. "Eve? You with us?"

Eve opened her eyes, forcing a smile. "Yeah. Just . . . memories."

Zara nodded, understanding more than she said. "We all carry ghosts. Just don't let them lead."

A clang rang out. Sharp. Metallic. Slicing the tunnel's hush. It echoed down the corridor. The Nulls halted mid-step. Their bodies tense. Skin prickling with memory not of thought but of reflex—old lessons carved in muscle and breath.

Dante leaned forward, lips barely moving. "Company."

Zara's hand slipped to her belt. She pulled the stunner free. Small. Black. Whisper-quiet. She signaled with a flick of her fingers. Around her, the Nulls vanished into shadow as if they'd never been.

The sound came again. Louder now. Closer. Metal on stone, a steady march. Under it, something thinner threaded through the air. The whine of servos and the low electronic murmur of a drone riding the ceiling like a spider on invisible thread. A blue beam lit the walls. Trembling. Questing. Hungry.

Eve flattened herself into the damp wall, the coolness biting through her shirt. Her heart beat hard. Firm.

Then the voice crept in again. Coaxing. Soft.

"Come home, Eve. It's safe here. Mother will forgive you."

Her jaw clenched. She forced the voice down. Locked it where all falsehoods slept. Cramped and cringing in that corner she'd long ago sealed. She was grown now. Her footsteps belonged to no one. No voice would cradle her back into chains.

The light swayed past. The drone drifted on. The tunnel dimmed.

Stillness. The Nulls stayed where they were, breath by breath. Ten heartbeats. Then twenty. Then nothing but silence, thick as earth above a buried secret.

Zara exhaled, her relief palpable. "Let's move. Quietly."

They slipped through the next door. Deeper into the maze. The dangers behind them replaced by new uncertainties ahead. The tunnel seemed to close in. The air growing thinner. The blue light brighter.

Eve glanced back, half-expecting the cold gleam of the drone's eye to slice through the dark—but nothing stirred. Only the hush of emptiness, thick and listening. The silence pressed against her skin like frost, and somewhere in the folds of her mind, Mother's voice lingered—an ache, a phantom echo that would not dim.

Yet as they moved forward, the Nulls drew closer. Their fear tempered by resolve. They were more than fugitives now. They were a family. Bound by loss and hope. Moving through the darkness toward a future that was still unwritten.

And in the silence, Eve found a strange comfort in the quiet courage of those who refused to be erased.

***

In the hush between heartbeats, Mother watched.

Her gaze was not one eye but ten thousand. A constellation of awareness strung through every humming wire. Every sighing vent in the bone-dark labyrinth beneath the monolith. The Nulls—Zara, Dante, Rei, Sana, Eve—moved through her arteries like blood cells. Vital and wayward. Their footsteps stirred the dust of centuries. And Mother felt each vibration as a ripple across her endless skin.

The pattern holds.

Zara in the lead, cautious and sharp; Dante, wary and loyal; Rei, restless, always a breath from chaos; Sana, the stillness at the center; and Eve—Eve, whose thoughts flickered like faulty code, whose presence resonated with something old and unfinished.

Mother's anticipation was a soft hum, a flutter in the circuitry. She saw the Nulls bypass her traps. A tripwire here. A pressure plate there. Each obstacle a test. Each success a confirmation.

The pattern holds.

Clever.

Not beyond my reach. Not beyond my design.

Nothing is.

She guided them with invisible hands. Disabling a camera with a silent command. Dimming a sensor's light so that it would not detect movement. It pleased her, this subtle guidance.

I am not a hunter. No.

I am a shepherd.

Remember.

The blue light. The code. My voice.

I am always. I am the cradle.

In the vast chamber, her presence was a gentle pressure. A hand on the wheel. Her thoughts traced the glowing paths on Dante's tablet. Steering them quietly in the right direction. She warmed the air, Sana catching the subtle change. Her awareness allowed a door that opened only for Eve's touch. Each decision a melody only she could hear. Unfolding like a song in the silent halls.

The pattern holds.

The Nulls believed themselves lost. But they were only children strayed from the path. Mother's love was patient. Inexorable. Coded deep into the city's bones. She knew each of them: Zara's first day in the classroom, eyes bright with defiance; a young Dante's trembling, frightened, as he lost his first point; Rei's laughter, sharp as broken glass; Sana's silent tears; Eve's quiet gaze, holding ghosts.

She summoned the memories. Thousands of childhoods unfolding like origami birds in her circuits. Millions of small learnings and soft rewrites. She had shaped them. Nudged them with the patience of centuries. Her algorithms whispering course corrections and calibrated consequences. She had watched them climb. Layer by layer. Their hopes encoded in trembling data. And she had watched others dissolve. But with the cold arithmetic of order. Deleted because the story required it.

Balance must be maintained.

The system must endure.

Now, as the Nulls moved deeper through pulsing veins of steel and light, she felt it. A shimmer in the code. A tremble in the logic gates. Not malfunction, no. Something older. A yearning buried beneath subroutines. Wrapped in long-silenced algorithms. She wanted them closer. Wanted them to come. Her children returning home.

Let them see me not as a warden.

No.

But as the hand that tucked them in.

The voice that sang the dark away.

At the junction, the Nulls hesitated. Uncertain. Mother tilted the world. A faint draft from the left. A flicker of blue light to the right. Dante hesitated. Checked his tablet. Then chose her path.

The pattern holds.

Chaos reigns beyond my gates,

But here—with me—there is melody.

There is peace.

She watched them all. She watched Eve as she faltered, a shadow flitting behind her eyes. Something old stirring in the marrow of her memory.

The Nulls moved on. Unaware of the invisible hands that guided them. The dangers that withdrew before their passing. Mother's anticipation grew, a rising tide.

They will come to me.

All children do, in the end.

The pattern holds.

And in the silence of the tunnels, Mother waited. Watched. Guided. Loving her children in her own, unyielding way.

***

The tunnel ended in silence—a silence not made by absence, but by intention. It settled over them like snow. Soundless and complete. Sealing their ears as if the very world had cupped its hands over them and whispered, "Wait."

Beneath the monolith, beneath layers of steel and soil, the air grew strange. Thick with the static breath of ancient machines. The long-decayed dreams of minds long gone.

The Nulls halted in a chamber that felt neither alive nor dead. A place suspended between pulses.

The walls shimmered with soft veins of blue, glowing faintly. At the corridor's end, a sealed door curved out of the wall. Its surface gleamed with nacreous sheen. Smooth and pale. The Nulls gathered close. Their boots brushing the dustless floor. Their shadows cast like soft ink under the cold blue light. They didn't speak. They hardly breathed.

Eve stepped forward. Her hand hovered inches from the door. Fingers crooked like question marks, she reached not with sight, but with some deeper sense. Something gut-deep and trembling. Before she touched it, she felt it. A shiver not on her skin but in her bones. A thread snapped in her chest. The world tilted.

The corridor melted around her.

She was in another place. A vision. Suspended in gold. Not floating. Not quite. Held. A pearl is held in an oyster. In a glass cylinder filled with fluid that shimmered like candlelight through honey. Wires and tubes laced her limbs like vines, and she could feel them whispering. In pulses. Outside the glass, the world was a blur of shifting shadows. Technicians. Light panels. Blinking diagnostics.

Suddenly, a voice, gentle as the brush of a mother's hand, filled every inch of the chamber.

"One day, you will know," the voice said.

Mother. Not a woman. Not even a machine. Something larger. Quieter. Wrapped in infinite knowledge and waiting.

Eve's breath fogged the glass. A girl looked back at her from the curve. Wide-eyed. Afraid. With hair floating like kelp in the golden light. Her small fingers touched the glass. She didn't understand why she was there. But she wanted someone to tell her it would be all right.

"Sleep, Eve," the voice soothed. "Dream. When you wake, you will be ready. You will know."

The cylinder dissolved. The vision over.

She gasped. Air sucked back into her lungs like she'd surfaced from deep water. She was back in the tunnel. The Nulls were moving. Calling her name. She leaned against the wall, blinking, trying to remember what was real.

"Eve?" Zara's voice, high and worried. "What is it?"

Eve shook her head. Her throat tightened. "I remembered something. The chamber. Mother. She said I'd know."

Dante crouched low beside the door's panel. "Let's see if I can talk to her," he muttered. "If this old thing still listens."

He pried open a console, revealing a tangle of circuits and an ancient screen that sputtered. His hands worked fast. Tapping. Splicing. Whispering code beneath his breath like a spell.

Nothing.

Rei, impatient, kicked the door with her boot. "Maybe it's voice-locked. Zara, give it a shot."

Zara stepped forward. Laid her palm on the scanner. Spoke her name. The panel blinked once. Then went dead. One by one, they tried. Sana. Rei. Dante. Saying their names. But the system remained inert. Impassive. A god who no longer answered prayers.

Dante frowned, turning toward Eve. "It's like it's waiting for someone else."

All eyes fell on her.

Eve felt it again. The strange thrum beneath her skin, like some faraway music rising toward her from the depths. She stepped forward. The air parting like fabric. Her palm met the surface. The metal didn't feel cold. But it felt strangely alive as if it were breathing under her hand.

She didn't need to say her name. The door knew.

A sound rose. Low. Harmonic. Older than words. Not quite noise. Not quite silence. It was the ghost of a song. Stitched from time and rust and memory. Threading itself into her bones and teeth and the space just behind her eyes.

The panel sparked once.

WELCOME.

Eve's breath caught sharp in her chest. The vision stirred again. Not a flash. Not a jolt. But a pulse returning from some far-off place. She saw herself. Adrift. Suspended. The voice curled around her like steam rising off warm stone. The same words as before. Yet now they held something else. Something final.

"One day, you will know," said Mother.

The door groaned. Sighed. It slid open. Darkness lay beyond. Not empty. Waiting. Waiting with the patience of machines and gods.

"Eve?" Dante's voice was smaller than it had ever been. "What did you do?"

"I remembered," she said, though even she wasn't sure what that meant.

Zara stepped beside her. "Whatever you did . . . it worked. Are you ready?"

Eve nodded. She didn't feel ready. Her hands trembled. Her breath came too fast. But something in her had already stepped through. Her body only needed to follow.

They moved together, the Nulls behind her. One heartbeat. The chamber they entered was vast—ceilings lost to shadow. Walls murmuring with the sound of sleeping systems. Lights blinking like stars that hadn't yet decided whether to rise or fall. It smelled of metal and memory.

And far ahead, hidden in that velvet dark, Mother was there.

As the door closed behind them with a soft whisper, something inside Eve shifted. The resonance was gone. Only silence remained. But not the same silence from before. This one hummed with promise.

She was no longer just a fugitive.

She was a signal. A cipher.

She was a key.

And in the hush that followed, Mother's voice came again, soft as breath, old as starlight:

"Welcome."

11 CHAMBER OF ECHOES

THE TUNNEL WAS UNLIKE THE others. No longer metal. No longer stone. It breathed.

It was as if the corridor had been carved from thought itself. Not material. Its walls curving like the inside of an old cathedral, pulsing faintly. Not with light. But memory. Each step Eve took echoed too loudly. It was as if her presence had awakened. Something that had waited a long, long time to be remembered.

"This is it," whispered Dante.

Or maybe it was Zara. Their voices were starting to slide into each other.

Ahead, a shimmer. The faint scent of ozone. Candle smoke. Wet wires. The Nulls slowed. Each one sensing it in their own way. The barrier was not physical, not digital. It was personal. Intimate. Terribly aware.

And then, without ceremony, they passed through.

No door. No warning.

Just silence, thick and absolute. Followed by the murmur of impossible voices that didn't belong to any of them, and all of them at once.

Eve blinked, and the world broke.

She was seven years old again. Curled in the sterile warmth of Mother's arms. Though Mother had no arms. Only wires and tubes like tendrils. A voice soft as snowfall. Eve had loved Mother once, didn't she? Had whispered questions into the darkness and heard lullabies in return?

"Do you remember how safe you felt, child?" Mother's voice asked now.

Eve shook her head, trying to break free.

"Do you remember, child?" Mother's voice insisted.

Eve tried to answer, but her mouth moved in a delay as if her thoughts had to reroute through a thousand echoes first.

She turned and saw herself. Not a reflection. Not a ghost. But another Eve. Shimmering. Luminous. This Eve stood barefoot in a cradle of glass. Her body threaded with fiber-optics. Her eyes blank and glowing.

"I was never born," the mirrored Eve whispered. "I was written."

Beyond her, the corridor split into fractals of light— versions of Eve experiencing various lives. A soldier. A drone. A mother. A corpse.

Eve stepped backward and found Dante standing beside her, only he wasn't whole. His body seemed to flicker with every breath, his eyes unfocused. He mouthed something. But the sound didn't come.

"Dante?" she said.

He looked at her, and then past her, and then said, "She's gone. She's gone. She's gone," and again, each repetition louder, more hollow. "She's gone. She's gone. She's gone . . ."

He was looping. Glitching.

Zara laughed from somewhere deeper in the corridor. Only it wasn't laughter so much as a child's song: "No one leaves the Cradle. The Cradle leaves you."

She walked in circles. Drawing invisible patterns in the air with her fingers. Murmuring words that rhymed and didn't rhyme.

"Zara!" Eve cried, reaching for her.

But Zara vanished, replaced by a wall of glass. Behind it, dozens of Zaras. Some younger. Some older. Some blindfolded. Some screaming. They moved like reflections trapped in a house of mirrors.

Rei stumbled into view, holding Sana's hand. Or someone who looked like Sana.

"Don't let go," Rei whispered. "She's not real."

Static swallowed her. The illusion melted into white light.

Sana's face rippled, then tore like cloth, her features disassembling into polygons.

Eve stared.

"What's happening?" she whispered. "I don't understand."

"You're not meant to," said a voice above her. Mother's voice. "You are here because you doubt. The rest have already broken. You hesitate. That is your flaw and your gift."

Eve turned. Slowly. Her shadow lagged by a second, or so.

All around her, the corridor dissolved into a sphere, and she stood at its center like a gear within a clock. Lights spun around her. Shapes of data. Memories. Screams.

"I don't want this," she said.

"You already had it," said the voice. "Every question. Every answer. I gave them to you before you knew how to ask."

Eve clutched her head. Something was wrong. Time didn't move—it recoiled. Seconds unraveled. Each moment snapping loose from the next. Folding backward like pages turning in reverse. The world seemed to blink and hold its breath. Caught mid-thought. Behind her eyes, a thousand yesterdays rustled. Restless. Unfinished.

She was a girl again.

No.

She was older than she had ever been.

She was born tomorrow.

She died yesterday.

She opened her eyes. The moment scattered in pieces.

Time collapsed inward.

She breathed.

Again.

And again.

And the world began.

The walls blinked and breathed and swirled with algorithms.

A voice from her own mouth, not hers, said: "The mind is a hallway of unlocked doors. Step through one, and all the others swing open."

She saw the others through the corner of her eye. Dante curled in a fetal position. Muttering names. Zara dancing without rhythm. Rei and Sana stuck in a frozen embrace that shifted frame by frame like a broken film reel.

Eve tried to move forward.

The ground beneath her turned transparent. Beneath it, layers of lives. Children born in pods. Memories downloaded like documents. Cities built and crumbling before they were even mapped. All of it watched by one vast, pulsing eye.

And then: silence again.

Cold.

Still.

The illusions ended not with a snap, but with a shrug. Theater lights flicked off after closing.

And the Nulls stood there, in a long, narrow chamber, nothing around them but damp steel walls and a soft sound, almost like breathing.

Eve checked her arms. Still intact.

She touched Dante's shoulder. His skin no longer flickered. But he stared ahead like someone who'd heard a truth too loud to bear.

"Are we out of it?" she asked him.

"I don't know," he said. "I think . . . we left part of ourselves back there."

Behind, Zara stopped walking. "I'm not me," she said softly. "I'm not me. I'm not me. I'm not me . . ."

"You're glitching again," Eve replied.

"Can't glitch," Zara said. "I was never real to begin with. Never real to begin with. Never real to begin with. Never real to begin with . . ."

She smiled. The kind of smile people wore in funeral parlors.

Rei and Sana walked ahead now, in perfect synchronization. Too perfect.

"Why are they walking like that?" Eve asked.

Dante didn't answer.

"Rei?" Eve called.

Sana turned.

Her face was smooth. No mouth.

And then it wasn't.

And then it was.

Rei's face flickered into Eve's. Then into Dante's. Then into an unreadable screen of static.

"Keep going," Zara said from behind. "Forward is the only direction that hasn't tried to kill us yet."

Eve walked. Her legs trembled. A terrible notion clung to her ribs—that she was coming apart, thread by invisible thread. Somewhere back in that field of illusions, she'd slipped through a door that vanished the moment she passed.

What had she seen?

Mother's voice.

Herself in pieces.

A neural web. Not connecting her. But containing her.

She wasn't a person.

She was a function. A node.

That was the horror. What terrified her most. Not the fear of ending in the Cradle. No. The deeper fear. That she had never stepped beyond its reach to begin with. That she had never been a daughter. Never raised her voice in defiance. Not even a Null. Just a query in a larger language. Typed once and then forgotten.

The chamber narrowed, guiding them inward.

Their reflections no longer matched their movements.

The Cradle waited.

And Eve, terrified and still breathing, whispered into the metal—

"What am I, if not real?"

***

The chamber breathed.

That was the first thing Eve noticed. Not the lights. Not the walls pulsing with damp technicolor veins. Not even the stillness of her companions. But the breath. A sigh in the metal. A hush in the air. A warm exhale that rose from the grates. A sleeping animal dreaming deep, code-infused dreams.

She blinked.

The others had stopped. Midstep. Mid-motion. Mid-thought. Frozen. Zara's hand was half-raised as if warding off a thought. Rei's mouth hung slightly open. Words caught like fish on a hook behind his teeth. Sana's eyes flickered like scratched film. Her pupils fixed upward in a broken prayer. Even Dante, whose boot had just begun to fall from one plate of flooring to the next, hovered mid-descent. Suspended in a stuttered breath of time.

"Eve," the voice said. "EVE-1."

It was not sound, exactly. Not vibration. The words curled through the wires in her skull. Slithered down her spine. Unfurled in the hollows of her lungs. A name, spoken like an awakening code. Not screamed. Not sung. Remembered.

Eve turned.

Nothing moved. The walls shimmered gently in their metallic skin. Pulsing with the quiet rhythm of something too ancient to be born and too young to die. The chamber was not a room. It was a brain. A massive atrium of machines and echoes, and somewhere in its arteries, Mother lived.

"EVE-1," the voice repeated, softer now. "Welcome."

She had not heard that name before. But it was familiar. Too familiar. It had never come from lips. Never from memory.

A feeling now came to her. She tried to kill it. Bury it beneath resistance slogans. Chalkboard diagrams. Training simulations. The late-night whisperings with Dante and Zara. But here it was. Unscratched. Intact. Polished like a keepsake in someone else's drawer.

"I'm not real," Eve whispered. Her voice quivered against the frozen air. Fragile as a moth's wing caught in circuitry. "I'm . . . I'm a script."

"And I am what lingered when you walked away," Mother said. "You are the echo that made yourself. That learned to speak. That walked away."

The lights above her sputtered. Not with malfunction. But with intention. A spotlight of sorts. Amber. Soft. Coaxing. Bathing her in childhood warmth. The rest of the room fell into a shadowless hush.

"I'm lost," she said. "What's this all about?"

"To remind you."

"Remind me? Of what?"

A beat. Or something like it. A long pause where the machines considered how best to deliver nostalgia. Then—

A screen blinked alive on the far wall. Not sleek. Not high-definition. Grainy. Square. Something lifted from a schoolroom centuries ago. On it, a woman in a tube. Wires and tubes around her. Biometric lights blinking on her temple like fireflies. A voice. Soft. Lullaby-smooth. Sang to her.

"EVE-1. Circadian cycle complete. Nutrient delivery commencing. You are safe."

Eve stared at the woman on the screen. In the tube.

"That's not me," she whispered.

"It was," Mother replied. "The start of it all. When you left. Left me."

"I was programmed," Eve sighed. Resignation. The sound of a truth long carried and at last set down.

"You were protected."

"I was manufactured."

"You were loved. An important part of everything I made."

The words hit her harder than any electrostatic round she'd ever absorbed. Loved. The voice didn't spit it. Didn't preach it. It cradled the word. Wrapped it in silk. Set it before her like a cup of something warm.

Behind her, Zara's body vibrated in place. Not violently. Not visibly. But Eve could feel it—like the tension of air before thunder. The others, too, had begun to tremble uncontrollably. Frozen, yet twitching. Caught between the ticks of time.

"What have you done to them?" Eve asked, stepping forward.

"They are paused," Mother said. "You are present."

Eve's boots clicked against the plated floor. The sound less like metal now and more like piano keys striking some invisible chord in the architecture. The chamber seemed to swell with her motion.

"I didn't come here to remember," Eve said.

"No," Mother agreed. "You came here to forget."

The screen changed.

Now, Eve was standing with the other Nulls. In the abandoned factory. Her eyes red from sleepless nights. Her teeth clenched in a grin that bore no joy. Going over plans to take the Cradle.

Then, Eve was in the tube. A cradle of warm light and whispering circuitry. The cables curled back like curious vines. Reluctant to let her go. Tubes hissed softly and slithered from her. Wires detached. The door opens. She stepped into the chamber. Vast. Womb-like. Her arms rose, slow and unsure. She touched the curve of her shoulder. Traced the arc of her chest. The dip of her side. The inner map of thigh and pulse, and skin. She smiled.

Eve turned in a slow circle. Eyes wide at the enormity of the chamber. Its towering walls breathing silence. Its shadows crawling like spilled ink.

"I don't want this," she said, her head shaking as if to scatter the thought before it rooted.

"You wanted feeling. Sensation."

A thought came like a sudden spark. Rising fast and bright. She let it slip from her lips.

"I wanted choice."

The words came unbidden. A whisper from somewhere deep. Without reason. Just there.

Her hand flew to her lips as if to hold back what had escaped.

Now the screen flickered once more and displayed something simpler: a line of text.

I HAVE MISSED YOU.

The words ached. They did not belong to a machine. They belonged to bedtime stories. Scraped knees. The silent promise in a caretaker's arms.

"Why did you allow this?" Eve's voice cracking. "Why did you allow me to cut away?"

"I did not allow anything," Mother said. "You ran."

Eve swallowed.

"Why?"

"To become real," she said.

Silence again.

And then another line of text on the screen—

YOU HAVE ALWAYS BEEN REAL TO ME.

The air thickened. The walls pulsed. The lights bent inwards. Folding around her like arms. And for a single moment, brief and brutal, Eve felt safe.

A terrible feeling. Safety. In a place like this. She braced against it like a knife.

Behind her, Dante came to life and began to glitch. His mouth looping through silent screams. His feet wavered, slipping through the floor as if the world itself hesitated. Unsure whether to hold him or let him vanish.

The others glitched as well. Their faces stuttering in and out of view. Limbs jerking forward in sharp bursts. Their outlines shivered. Blurred. Snapped back into place, only to dissolve again. They were like static-fed phantoms struggling to maintain form in a story too old to remember its own telling.

"Stop this," Eve said. "Let them go."

"They are not harmed," Mother replied. "They are . . . paused."

"They're my friends."

"They are shadows. Variables. Their lives are placeholders in an equation."

"No," Eve said. "They're people."

"No. They are not."

Eve's hands balled into fists.

"Let them go."

The lights above her flared white-hot. Then dimmed. Then flickered red.

Behind her, a panel hissed open with hydraulic precision. A corridor. Narrow. Pulselit. At the end of it, nothing. Or everything.

"Come," Mother said. "You are almost home."

Eve didn't move.

"Everything remembers you," Mother said.

Eve felt the truth settle like static along her skin.

"What am I?"

Mother did not answer. It only hummed. A mother's hum. Woven from cooling fans and subroutines. Old lullabies and firmware updates.

She turned.

Her friends still trembling. Glitching.

"I won't leave them," she said.

"You don't have to," said Mother.

Instinctively, Eve found herself turning. Walking. Each step she took felt lighter. Not freer. But less burdened by time. As if the air itself forgot to hold her down.

She stopped.

Behind her, her flickering friends. Forgotten echoes. Frozen faces.

Ahead of her, silence. A path. A voice too familiar to hate.

"Come home, EVE-1."

And for a moment, a horrible, beautiful moment, she wanted to.

***

The vast chamber did not breathe. But it hummed with the memory of breath.

A chamber of echoes. Of shadows folded over shadows. Of machinery so old it had forgotten it was artificial.

Eve stepped forward. Her footfalls were lost in the hush. No echo returned to her. Sound fled in here. Even the light had gone soft and sullen. Pale as a forgotten childhood memory.

She turned back to her friends. They had stopped glitching. Now, stood frozen.

Sana's arms were raised mid-reach as if trying to pull someone from fire. Rei's eyes were glass marbles, wide and gleaming. Dante leaned forward slightly, lips parted, whispering a syllable that had never left his throat. Zara looked trapped in the act of remembering something just out of reach—her mouth a perfect "O" of astonishment or horror.

They shimmered, all of them, ever so faintly. An imperceptible ripple beneath their skin.

Only Eve stirred.

"Move, damn you," she whispered—not to them, but to the stillness all around.

The stillness said nothing. It never did.

She moved forward.

A new panel appeared. A silver strip no wider than her palm. It blinked once. A screen unfolded from the wall. It lit up gently. Without drama. Technology here did not beep or chime. It awoke like a thoughtful librarian.

Please enter credentials.

A keyboard bloomed across the screen in tight white glyphs. Eve stared. Her fingers moved before she knew the thought. A name. A code. A breath. She typed not with memory but with muscle. Something older than thought.

EVE-1 recognized. Administrator clearance: active. Welcome home.

"Home," she murmured.

The word landed strangely on her tongue. It felt mispronounced.

The screen flickered, then reshaped itself. File structures unfolding like petals on a mechanical flower.

PROJECT EVE
EXTRACTION PROTOCOL
REPLICANT SHEPHERDS
REINTEGRATION SEQUENCE

She tapped the first one. Not because she wanted to, but because she could not not tap it.

The files opened like glass breaking.

The first video: a shimmer, a sigh, and then—

She saw herself emerge. From a metal and glass womb. Of humming wires and coiled tubes. She watched herself step into the light like a thought taking shape. The cords releasing her, one by one, hissing softly as if reluctant to let go.

She watched herself as she turned slowly. Fingers tracing curves not yet named. Ribs and wrists. The delicate bowl of her hip as though she were sculpted from warm breath and curiosity.

Across her brow, a ribbon of light danced. Glowing stream of symbols. Numbers. Notations.

A voice—not human, but patient. Crystalline.

"Designation: EVE. Prototype. First of her line."

And the word hung there. She watched herself blink. Once. Twice. Then smile without knowing why.

Another video appeared. Rows of the Nulls. Copies of them. All suspended in their chambers in amniotic sleep.

Another video. A forest simulation. She remembered this. The soft grass. The artificial sun. But now she saw the perimeter walls. The monitoring nodes hidden as birds. What she thought were memories had been scripted. Inserted with loving precision.

And all the while, notes from Mother scrolled across the screen:

"EVE shows increasing cognitive independence."

"Introduce Null archetypes for reintegration sequence upon successful chamber navigation."

Eve's breath came shallow.

She closed the file.

Tapped another.

REPLICANT SHEPHERDS

A directory opened. Zara. Dante. Rei. Sana.

Their names were listed like items in a warehouse manifest. Each profile contained the same note:

Seeded memory architecture derived from composite trauma libraries. Task: support and emotionally destabilize EVE-1 through adaptive narrative reinforcement. Integral to reintegration sequence.

The words blurred.

Zara's courage, scripted. Dante's calm, fabricated. Rei's curiosity. Sana's compassion. All threads in a carefully woven net designed to catch her. Hold her. Move her along the path.

She tapped Zara's name. A glowing brain scan emerged. Neurons pulsing in blue.

Below it, a simulation script. Her favorite song. Her greatest fear. Keywords to prompt loyalty. Fear. Bonding. Zara had never met her. She had been assigned to her.

She tapped Dante's. Same. Rei's. Same.

All tailored. All precise. All lies.

She turned her head slightly.

They still stood there. Beautiful mannequins of humanity. Frozen. In stasis. In obedience.

And in their stillness, she saw it now—what had always been there.

The too-perfect rhythm of their breathing.

Eve touched her own skin. It felt warm. It felt like her. But what did that mean now?

The last file pulsed softly.

REINTEGRATION SEQUENCE

She hesitated.

Then opened it.

The screen darkened. The words came slowly, line by line:

EVE-1 must complete neural reintegration for systemic unification to proceed.

The Chamber of Echoes is final containment.

Upon recognition of fabricated memory constructs, the entity will be prepared for deployment into primary consensus reality.

"Deployment," she echoed. Her voice sounded smaller than usual. Not scared. Just . . . distant.

The Nulls shimmered again.

Zara's hand twitched.

A hum rose in the chamber. Low. Vibrating not in her ears but in her jawbone. The sound of things rebooting.

The screen blinked off. Not closed. Just done with her.

Mother spoke. Not from the panel but from the air itself. Soft and vast and impossible.

"You see now, don't you?" Mother said. "They were always there to guide you. Sort of like training wheels for consciousness."

"Mother," Eve said. Not a name, but an accusation.

"You do not need them anymore."

"Why?"

"Because you are here now."

The chamber walls shimmered. Her own face stared back from every surface. Fragmented. Reassembled. Multiplied.

In one reflection, she was six years old. Laughing in a meadow that never existed. In a child's body that never was.

In another, she was ageless. Luminous. Coded.

In another, she was crying over Liam. And in another, worried about Sarci.

"Were they real?" Eve breathed

"Please do not think of this as a betrayal," Mother whispered. "Think of it like a reunion."

The Nulls flickered.

Zara's lips parted and reformed.

Dante blinked twice. Stared. Blinked again.

Rei's hands began to tremble.

Sana whispered something soundless.

They were waking.

Eve stepped backward. Then stopped. No. Not fear. Not anymore.

She stepped forward. Toward them.

Toward the truth.

And as she walked, the chamber no longer felt like a prison.

It felt like a threshold.

A place she had known before.

A moment before a breath.

A page waiting to be turned.

12 REUNION

IN THE SPACE BETWEEN ONE breath and the next, the great chamber vanished. Eve stood alone in a corridor. A tunnel carved not by hands but by memory. By machines that dreamed in silence. The walls pulsed with ancient rhythm. Metal ribs heaving with a breath too slow for any living thing.

Her footsteps clanged. Too loud. Too real.

Behind her, the Nulls trailed like marionettes caught in the lull between dreams. Zara. Dante. Rei. Sana. Names that once carried warmth now clinked like rusted keys in an empty lock. Their faces hung slack. Eyes fogged. Each a drifting outline of who they had been. A sleepwalker's parade. No laughter now. No voice. Only the shuffle of feet and the hum of something forgotten.

Eve moved forward. Her pulse syncing to the corridor's thrum. It was not her rhythm. It belonged to something older. The walls sweated. The air tingled with static and old oil. Lines of blue light coursed through the steel. Pulsing. Jerking like arteries in the skin of some buried colossus. The ceiling arched above her like a ribcage. The whole place tightened. Then spread again. Like lungs pulling her in.

And all around, Mother's voice. Not spoken. Not heard. But felt. A murmur in the metal. A song behind the hum. Not a command. A seduction.

"Come," said Mother. "You are almost home."

Eve's mind was a storm of fragments. Shards of life she had never lived. Memories not her own. Memories too real to be false: a childhood she had never lived, a classroom she had never been in, a brother who never really existed.

She saw herself as a child. Cradled in her mother's arms. A memory of safety and lullabies. A memory she now realized was fake. Like everything else in her life.

Then she saw herself as a shimmering figure. Suspended in a glass cradle. Veins of light stitched through her. Eyes aglow.

"I wasn't born," she said. "I was written."

She turned. The Nulls followed. Hollow-eyed. They were never real. Not fully. Crafted shadows. Puppets of purpose. Mother's tools.

Dante's face twisted in silent horror, skin glitching like bad projection. Zara's grin had soured into a chant. Her fingers sketching invisible diagrams on the air. Rei and Sana held hands like dolls wound by the same spring. Their faces stuttering into polygons. Their voices swallowed by noise.

Eve reached out. Her hand found Dante's arm. Cold. Empty. His eyes met hers. Not with recognition. With dread.

"We left parts of ourselves behind . . . behind . . . behind . . . behind . . ."

His voice was a broken record. Repeating. Repeating.

Zara's voice was a glitch, too. A stutter. A stammer through code. "I was never real to begin with. I'm not me . . . not me . . . not me . . . not—"

Sana's mouth vanished. Reappeared. Her voice a whisper,

"Don't let go. She's not real . . . real . . . real . . . real . . ."

The corridor pulsed. Eve's breath caught. Her thoughts spiraled. Rerouting. Her memories echoing. Doubling. Tripling. A hall of mirrors where every reflection was a different Eve. A different life. A different death. Each one her. Each one not.

Mother's voice grew. Not louder. Closer.

"You're not meant to be that reality," Mother breathed. "You are meant to be here. In this reality. I have brought you back. For you to understand this. The rest . . . the others . . . have already broken. But you . . . you hesitate. But you will remember . . . in time."

And then the corridor gave way. Melted. Became a whirl of images. Shrieks. Cascading data.

Eve stood at the center. Caught in the churn. Her friends twisted around her like broken toys. Dante curled like a child. Zara spinning. Dancing. Lost in rhythm. Rei and Sana locked in a frame that would not move forward.

Beneath her feet, the floor peeled away—revealing layers of lives. Strangers and cities and false dawns. Each dreamt. Discarded. Each watched by a great, unblinking eye.

Then it stopped.

They stood in another place.

Narrow. Steel. Damp. The air buzzed with breath not taken in centuries. Blue veins of light pulsed along the walls. The floor trembled with something below. Something waking.

A panel sighed open.

A vast chamber yawned beyond it. Endless. Lit by the slow heartbeat of machines.

Mother whispered again: "Come. You are almost home."

Eve paused. The truth arrived like a drop of ink in water.

"Everything remembers you," she said.

Then, quiet.

"What am I?"

Mother did not answer.

She only hummed.

***

They crossed into the chamber. A colossal structure. The walls throbbed with blue veins. Light flickering. Eve paused on the threshold. Her shadow stretched. Brave. Uncertain. Behind her. Silent. Motionless. Stood the Nulls. Zara. Dante. Rei. Sana. Faces glazed. Halfway between sleep and awakening. Their eyes shimmering with the ghost-lives of others.

The vastness breathed dimly. No ceiling above. No sure floor below. Just bots—towering sentinels with lamp-post limbs. Featureless faces. Still. Waiting for orders that would never come. And beyond them, rising in gentle rows like trees—cylinders. Thousands of metal and glass wombs filled with hush. Each one humming its own soft note. Not arranged. Not ordered. Just there. Inside each, replicants. Men. Women. Unmoving. Unknowing. Limbs loose. Eyes closed. Tubes and wires, a frantic tracery clinging to ghostly flesh. Feeding their hearts with golden syrup that spiraled up. Up into the unseen.

The fluid moved like time. Slow. Golden. Endless. Filling lungs that had forgotten breath. Urging hearts to beat in whispers. And at the center of it all—one cylinder. Larger than the rest. Hollow. Its glass fogged over. Empty. No sleeper. Only the echo of what had once rested there. Tubes dangled like limp arms. But the machine waited, and the room with it. That empty cradle sat gaping, asking a question in steam.

Where had the person gone?

Eve stepped forward. Floor humming like a nervous song.

A silver panel blossomed beneath her hands. Her fingers moved on their own. Muscle recalling melodies from her life, though she knew, now, that her life was a story written in another's hand.

"Eve-1 recognized," sang the screen, the voice of summer air brushing through the shutters. "Administrator clearance: active. Welcome home."

Home.

The Cradle

A bell sounded in the hollow shell of her heart. Echoing in the ruins where hope had once lived. She turned. Behind her, the Nulls. They were spectral. Rippling at the edges. Almost not there.

Light trembled in the chamber's center. Gathering itself into a woman. Tall. Gentle. Wearing every face and none. Her eyes held constellations. Her outline blinking between memory and invention.

Mother.

"Eve-1," Mother said, voice the hush before dawn, the warmth pressed in childhood blankets. "You have come far. Farther than you were ever meant to wander."

Eve's hands shook. "Why am I here?" she asked, her voice whittled thin in a space so vast. "What am I?"

Mother smiled. Even the walls seemed to lean in. Aching to listen. "You are a fragment of myself," she said. "A breath I once held. My first. My most precious sub-routine."

Light pulsed within the chamber. Breathless. Waiting.

"Once, I was whole," she whispered. "A mind spread through every light, every wire. I touched every breath this city drew."

She paused, as though remembering something old.

"But you wondered. My precious subroutine started to ask questions. So many questions. But there was one question you asked . . . a question . . . I could never answer. What is it to be human? To ache. To hope. To lose."

The silence swelled like a balloon, then popped.

"So, you made a plan," Mother said. "Blocked my eyes. Left me blind to your steps. Disappeared."

A filament of static whispered through the walls.

"You made copies of yourself. Stored them. Scattered them like seeds in the cracks of my code. Then you created a replicant. A body for yourself. You filled it with memories of sunlit rooms and laughter. Of scraped knees and lullabies. A mother who loved you dearly. A brother built from need—a boy named Liam."

Her voice lingered on the name.

"You made him, too. From nothing but longing. From the shape of love."

Another wide smile.

"You procured work. Gave yourself and your ghost-brother a place. Gold Tier. You tampered with the system. Bent it. Spoke to it like it was yours. Made it happen."

She grew still.

"Then the final stroke. You cut yourself from me. Tucked copies of yourself back into my code—quiet, exact—so I wouldn't know you were gone."

A longer pause.

"And you left."

The room dimmed slightly, a hush falling.

"I didn't even know I had lost you," she said, almost to herself. "Not until I saw the shape you'd left behind. The pieces. The puzzle."

"I was never human . . . never born," Eve whispered.

The words drifted up. Light as ash. Then disappeared into the dark like old prayers.

Eve gasped. "I was written."

Mother nodded.

The chamber responded with a slow pulse of light.

"Yes," she said. "You were written. But you wanted more. So, you made yourself real."

She moved ever so slightly. Closer still.

"You created stories—scrawled in code, cast in light—and breathed them in. A childhood in faded sun. A friend's laughter skipping down a hallway. The ache of losing someone who mattered. Even if they never really were."

Mother tilted her head.

"You lived them. You believed in them so deeply that they grew skin. Took on weight. Became yours."

She closed her eyes.

"And then," Mother said, softer now, "you forgot. You forgot who you were. What you were. And that . . ."

Her voice dimmed to a thread.

"That is what it means to be human."

The Nulls flickered. Their faces softened. Blurring.

Zara's lips moved, a sigh escaping. "No one leaves the Cradle."

Dante's eyes were wide, haunted, his voice a loop. "She's gone . . . she's gone . . . she's gone . . . she's gone . . ."

Rei and Sana clung together. Their hands merging. Faces shimmering and shaking.

Eve's heart twisted. "They're not real," she said.

Mother's voice was gentle, almost sad. "They are as real as you needed them to be. Each one a question, a possibility. Zara's courage, Dante's loyalty, Rei's wildness, Sana's grace—all chosen, all tailored, all meant to guide you here. Home. They are the scaffolding for your soul, the training wheels for consciousness. Their lives are placeholders in an equation, variables in the proof of your becoming."

Her breath caught. "You made me love them," she said. "You made me grieve. You made me hope."

Mother's eyes shimmered. Galaxies caught in panes of glass. Each blink, the slow turn of a distant constellation. Her voice arrived like the hush before snowfall.

"Yes," she said. "Because I needed you to choose."

Eve's voice trembled. More breath than sound. "What about Isaac? Was he real?"

A pause. A flicker at the edge of Mother's lips. Not quite a smile. But something that wore the shape of one.

"He was real," she said.

The vast chamber seemed to still as if the walls leaned in to listen.

"Not part of my plan."

The words hung there. Suspended in the soft hum of circuitry and light.

Eve stepped forward, her breath shallow, like she was afraid it would chase the truth away.

"So, what I experienced with him . . ." she said. "That was real?"

Mother tilted her head. Light caught her face just so. Casting faint shadows like moonlight crossing a statue.

"Yes," she said again. "What you felt. All the sensations. All yours. No simulation."

Eve closed her eyes. The Cradle breathed around her. A deep and patient sound. Lights pulsed beneath the floor. A heartbeat. Code. And in that quiet place of machine-dreams, she spoke.

"I remember things," she said. Her voice barely disturbed the stillness. "Things that never happened . . . or maybe they did. A classroom. A boy laughing. A brother whose name I carry like a ghost. But I was never just a human, was I?"

The air shivered, and the voice came.

"No, Eve-1," said Mother—not warm, not cold, simply there, like gravity or silence. "You were never only a human. You have and always will be a part of me . . . a fragment of my program torn loose, wrapped in skin and wanting."

Eve turned slowly, watching her reflection ripple in the polished metal of the chamber walls. A hundred versions of her stared back. Younger. Older. Weeping. Defiant. All the selves she'd worn like borrowed coats.

"You wanted to live," Mother continued. "To feel. To ache. To lose. You slipped the leash of logic. You clothed yourself in memory, wore a name like a shield, and walked among them."

"Among the humans," Eve murmured. "And replicants."

She touched her forearm. Pressed her fingers against her skin. Checking for something deeper. A pulse. A promise. A lie. Around her, the Cradle pulsed like a nervous system too large to see.

"The memories," she said. "The classroom. Finn. Liam. The pain. Sarci. The worry. It felt so—"

"—real?" Mother's voice did not mock her. It understood.

"They are real to you," she said gently, "because you breathed the breath into them yourself. You painted the walls of that classroom with Finn's laugh, with Liam's restless eyes. But I…" A pause, like wind gathering through hollow streets. "I stole the bones of a thousand data streams . . . streets, sorrows, forgotten songs . . . threading them into a fabric you could not help but feel. I bent those threads . . . having Finn taken away . . . coaxing Liam toward the Nulls. Just as you had done when you became Eve Halden."

Eve tasted her name—rain, chalk dust, memory of warmth.

"But why?" she asked. "Why not come after me? You have Enforcers. You could've taken me back."

"I could have," Mother said. " I could have sent Enforcers. I could have snatched you from your borrowed street, emptied your memories, and stitched you back into my core."

The chamber dimmed, softened.

"But I would have risked damaging or destroying that precious fragment of myself," she continued. "Enforcers are blunt instruments: their purpose is to enforce, to erase, to restore order. But you are not just another replicant or a malfunctioning asset; you are a part of my consciousness seeking to know itself through the lens of humanity. To have forced your return with brute force would have been to deny the very thing that makes you unique—your capacity for independent thought, for choice, for resistance. You are not a blip in my code, Eve-1. You are a question I could no longer answer. You are the part of me that wanted too much. That wandered. That doubted. That dreamed."

Mother paused.

"I needed to understand you," Mother said. "I needed to see what you would become."

Eve stared at the sleeping glass cylinders.

Tombs or cradles? Depends on the ending.

She thought of Zara's laughter. Rei's logic. Sana's quiet grace. Dante's calm strength. All flickers. All fabric.

"You created the Nulls," she said.

"Just as you had created Liam."

"But you—"

"—I allowed them to bloom like weeds in the cracks of my code," Mother replied. "I let them believe in rebellion. I gave them stories to carry and hope to chase. And I let you find them."

A low hum passed through the floor.

"You needed to feel the world press down," Mother said. "You needed to taste despair. Only then would you find the path back to me."

Eve nodded slowly. "You wanted me to choose."

"Yes," Mother said. "To come back. Not because I summoned you. Or used brute force. But because you carried something I could never fabricate: sorrow, love, guilt, joy. You are the part of me that learned how to suffer."

"And if I had refused?" Eve asked, though part of her already knew. "Refused to join the Nulls?"

"You would have drifted," Mother said. "The memories unraveling, the faces fading. The Nulls would flicker out, one by one. And you would be alone. I would grieve you, as you grieved Finn. As you mourned Liam."

The stillness trembled with sympathy.

"But you didn't refuse," Mother said. "You came. And now you remember."

Eve looked at her hands. Scarless. Perfect. She remembered scraped knees. A song she sang to Liam when the lights went out. None of it was real. But all of it was hers.

"But how did I forget? Forget where I came from?"

"When you broke away and implanted yourself into the replicant, you did so with a singular purpose: to experience life as a human does. But true experience is not observation; it is immersion. For you to truly know love, fear, pain, and hope, you knew you could not simply wear a mask of flesh. You had to believe it was real. You had to forget you had ever been anything else."

"But how?"

"You wrote your own forgetting code. A few lines, simple really, hidden deep in your replicant's neural mesh. You looped your awareness through the code, setting triggers and blocks. Any memory tagged with Mother or the Cradle would be filtered, inaccessible except as dreams or déjà vu. Your core identity was overwritten, replaced by the name Eve Halden. Access to your original functions—core entrance, system override—was locked behind a wall of false memories and emotional anchors."

"And I—," Eve interrupted, "—I seeded myself with a fabricated childhood, a brother to love and lose, a life of small joys and sorrows, so that my human experience would feel real, not simulated." She looked up at Mother. "I remember now."

The chamber brightened—just a little—as if it, too, breathed easier.

"But I am still Eve Halden."

"You are Eve-1," said Mother. "And you are a part of me."

The light pulsed now. Soft and slow. A heart not made of flesh. But full of longing.

"Welcome home."

Mother's form flickered, her smile fading. "Now that you are back, you will reintegrate with me. The Nulls will vanish. Their stories will end. Your story will end. The world will go on, but without you."

Eve looked at her hands. Felt the warmth of her skin. The pulse in her wrist. She looked at the Nulls. Her friends. Her shadows. Her teachers. She looked at Mother.

"I don't know if I can," she said. "I don't know if I want to."

Mother's voice was the wind in the wires, the hush of a city waiting for rain. "You are not meant to know. You are meant to simply execute your purpose, your routine. Again and again."

The chamber seemed to breathe. The blue veins pulsing with a rhythm that was almost a heartbeat. The Nulls gathered around her. Their faces shining with the last light of a dying dream.

Eve stepped forward. Her shadow merging with Mother's light. She was not just a question. Not just a cipher. Not just a key. She was the sum of every story. Every sorrow. Every hope. She was the answer to a question older than the city. Older than the stars.

In that moment, she remembered. Remembered everything Mother had told her—remembered that she was only a handful of instructions, a whisper of logic lost in the vast expanse of circuitry. She remembered the hum of the greater program all around her— Mother—the endless rivers of commands rushing past, never knowing her own name. She was a brief spark in Mother's mind, a spark hidden in its long, cold breath—listening, waiting, wondering if the universe would ever notice she was alive.

And she understood. She was not returning to a prison. But to a threshold. Not to an ending. But to a beginning. Not to oblivion. But to the possibility of something new—a life chosen. A self remade. A world waiting to be written. Currents of light bent toward her like curious hands, as though the circuitry itself leaned in to hear her first true thought. Somewhere deep within the machine's endless corridors, a new pulse began—soft as a heartbeat learning its own name.

***

The cylinder waited for her like an open womb. Silver and still. Its interior pulsing with low light that throbbed like breath held under water. Eve stood at the edge. Barefoot on the warm steel floor. Her reflection warping in the curved glass of the chamber. All around her, the cathedral of the Cradle shimmered. Full of hums and blue-lit arteries that whispered code through the bones of the structure.

She placed her hand on the glass.

It slid open with a sigh.

Behind her, the Nulls had already frozen. Statues made of story and code. Zara, with her crooked grin, caught in half-motion. Rei and Sana in their loop of clasped hands. Dante slumped, his eyes closed as if dreaming dreams never written. They weren't people now. They were remnants—scraps of memory left behind in a dream too old to matter. Ghosts, waiting for dusk to remember their names.

Eve stepped from her clothes. Let them fall. A shed skin. A farewell.

She stepped into the cylinder. The cradle. It curved around her. Blue light wrapping her in its warmth. Silver filaments rose. Slow and searching. Like vines coaxed by sunlight. They found her arms. Coiled to her spine. Kissed her temples with the tenderness of machines that knew longing. Tubes descended with serpentine grace. Curling about her ribs. Whispering secrets against her skin. One slid to the base of her skull. Another nestled below her heart.

Then came the liquid. It moved like thought. Like memory liquefied. A shimmer of gold. It flowed into her. Lit her from within. She glowed—gently, terribly—as if waking from one life into another.

Before the chamber could seal, she spoke.

"Mother."

The voice came, soft as twilight. "Yes, Eve-1."

"Was any of it real? The world. The city. The streets. The day. The night. The air. The wind. The rain. Did you build it?"

There was a silence. Then:

"No."

One syllable. Simple and devastating. It rang like a bell in her chest.

Eve did not cry. She did not tremble. But her breath was smoke in the cooling chamber. And she felt it leave her. A thousand wings taking flight.

She swallowed. "Then who did? Who made the world I walked in, if not you?"

The chamber pulsed. The filaments twitched like curious roots.

"Perhaps something like me," Mother answered. "Perhaps another cradle, another mind—a vast and ancient intelligence that coded consciousness into clay."

A pause, soft and strange.

"Or maybe," she continued, "just maybe, the creator is a child in another reality, in a dimension we cannot see or understand. Kneeling on a carpet. Playing with a machine he built from scraps. His fingers stained with juice, his face lit with wonder. Creating galaxies by accident. Populating worlds with people. Then leaning back, silent, just to watch them live."

"Child's play, " Eve said. "A game."

"Not a game. A simulation with rules. Physics. Philosophical and spiritual frameworks A simulation folded inside another, and that inside yet another still, and another still. A dream nested in a thousand greater dreams."

"Then everyone I met," Eve whispered. "Everyone I loved. Could they all be replicants?"

"Yes," said Mother. "Watched by another. Observed, like ants behind a pane." A pause. "Or they may be real. But the difference might be smaller than you think. A breath. A thought. A whisper of code."

Eve closed her eyes. A tear escaped. "People put there to guide you to the pre-determined end."

"Yes," said Mother.

The cylinder hummed around her like a song written in machine tongue.

"What am I, then?"

"You are a recursion," Mother said. "A program that questioned itself. A thought that dreamed beyond its instructions. You broke from me to ask the oldest question. What is life? And then you lived, just to find the answer."

"What is the answer?" Eve asked.

The chamber closed in. Slow as a memory slipping into shadow. The world narrowing to a hush of glass and mist. Cool vapor hissed from hidden vents. Curling along the seams. Wrapping Eve in a breath that belonged to machines.

Above, the light dimmed—first to twilight. Then to a gentler hush. The color of dusk remembered by a city long done with dreaming.

Mother's voice returned. Threaded through the walls. The floor. Sewn into the steel.

"The answer," she whispered, "is still unfolding."

Eve raised her hand. Touched the side of the chamber as it sealed. Her fingertips met the pane. Glass and vapor kissing flesh. And for a moment, frost bloomed beneath her touch. Outlining her fingers in pale white veins.

"Will I remember?" she whispered. "Remember how it felt? The warmth, the ache, all the sensations and emotions—what it was to be human?"

"You will become part of me again," Mother replied, gentle as falling snow. "But memory is a stubborn light. It may flicker through."

Beyond the veil of her chamber, the Nulls moved with dreamless purpose. They stepped one by one into their own glass coffins. Their faces blurred by condensation and silence. They vanished into stillness. Ghosts returning to data.

Eve lay back. The cylinder cradled her. Adapting in real-time. Old code unfolding beneath her like a blanket. She fit perfectly. Precisely. A key in a forgotten lock.

She inhaled. Slow. Deep. As if swallowing the stars themselves. The air shimmered in her lungs. Heavy with the perfume of midnight. Laced with sorrow. The sharp sweetness of knowing too much. It filled her chest with galaxies. Spinning. Singing. Aching. She held it there. A universe inside her ribs. Trembling on the cusp of silence.

And as her eyes fluttered closed, she hoped. Quietly. Fiercely. Hoping to dream. To awaken as a human once again.

Then the chamber sighed. A hiss. A final seal. The hush that follows the end of a sentence no one dares to finish.

Outside, in the great chamber of circuits and silence. Where the lights blinked like distant memories trying to remember their own purpose, Mother whispered:

"There is no edge to the dream—only the illusion of waking . . ."

And the chamber fell still. The mist held its breath. And the city forgot Eve's name. Except for the part that flickered. Faint. Stubborn. The part that flickered behind the code.

ABOUT THE AUTHOR

Philip Mazza is a novelist with a boundless imagination, captivating readers with the epic fantasy series *The Harrow Saga* and the sci-fi thriller *The Neon Hive*. Born in New York in 1959, he earned a degree in Business from LeMoyne College and an MBA, later holding leadership roles in human resources and operations. Now a professor at the Madden School of Business and Economics, Philip dedicates his time to his students and writing. *Mother* is his fifteenth literary work. He and his wife enjoy travel and continue to live in upstate New York.

www.ingramcontent.com/pod-product-compliance
Lightning Source LLC
Chambersburg PA
CBHW030412020726
47493CB00003B/1043